P9-DMU-720

THE
INVASION

<JOIN THE FIGHT>

ANIMORPHS™

THE INVASION
THE VISITOR
THE ENCOUNTER

ANIMORPHS™

THE
INVASION

K. A. APPLEGATE

SCHOLASTIC INC.

NEW YORK   TORONTO   LONDON   AUCKLAND
SYDNEY   MEXICO CITY   NEW DELHI   HONG KONG

For Michael

If you purchased this book without a cover, you should be aware that this book is stolen property. It was reported as "unsold and destroyed" to the publisher, and neither the author nor the publisher has received any payment for this "stripped book."

No part of this publication may be reproduced, stored in a retrieval system, or transmitted in any form or by any means, electronic, mechanical, photocopying, recording, or otherwise, without written permission of the publisher. For information regarding permission, write to Scholastic Inc., Attention: Permissions Department, 557 Broadway, New York, NY 10012.

ISBN 978-0-545-29151-4

Copyright © 1996 by Katherine Applegate

All rights reserved. Published by Scholastic Inc. SCHOLASTIC, ANIMORPHS, and associated logos are trademarks and/or registered trademarks of Scholastic Inc.

12 11 10 9 8 7 6 5 4 3 2 1   11 12 13 14 15 16/0

Printed in the U.S.A.   40

This edition first printing, May 2011

CHAPTER 1

My name is Jake. That's my first name, obviously. I can't tell you my last name. It would be too dangerous. The Controllers are everywhere. Everywhere. And if they knew my full name, they could find me and my friends, and then . . . well, let's just say I don't want them to find me. What they do to people who resist them is too horrible to think about.

I won't even tell you where I live. You'll just have to trust me that it is a real place, a real town. It may even be *your* town.

I'm writing this all down so that more people will learn the truth. Maybe then, somehow, the human

1

race can survive until the Andalites return and rescue us, as they promised they would.

Maybe.

My life used to be pretty normal. Normal, that is, until one Friday night at the mall. I was there with Marco, my best friend. We were playing video games and hanging out at this cool store that sells comic books and stuff. The usual.

Marco and I had run out of quarters for the games, right when he was ahead by a lot of points. Mostly, we're equally good at games. I have a system at home so I get lots of practice time in, but Marco has this amazing ability to analyze games and figure out all the little tricks. So sometimes he beats me.

Or maybe I just wasn't concentrating very well. I'd had kind of a bad day at school. I'd tried out for the basketball team and I didn't make the cut.

It was no big deal, really. Except that Tom—he's my big brother—he was this total legend on the junior high basketball team. Now he's the main scorer for the high school team. So everyone expected me to make the team, easy. Only I didn't.

Like I said, no big thing. But it was on my mind, just the same. Lately, Tom and I hadn't been hanging out as much. Not like we used to. So I figured, you know, if I got his old position on the team . . .

Well, anyway, we were out of money and getting ready to head home when we ran into Tobias. Tobias was . . . I mean, I guess he still *is* kind of a strange guy. He was new at school, and he wasn't the toughest kid around, so he got picked on a lot.

I actually met Tobias when he had his head in a toilet. There were these two big guys holding him down and laughing while they flushed, sending Tobias's straggly blond hair swirling around the bowl. I told the two creeps to back off, and ever since then, Tobias figured I was his friend.

"What's up?" Tobias asked.

I shrugged. "Not much. We're heading home."

"Out of quarters," Marco commented. "Certain people keep forgetting that the SleazeTroll shows up right after you cross the Nether Fjord. So certain people keep losing the game — and losing our quarters." Marco kept jerking his thumb at me, just in case Tobias couldn't figure out who he meant by "certain people."

"So, like, maybe I'll walk home with you guys," Tobias said.

I said sure. Why not?

We were heading for the exit when I spotted Rachel and Cassie. Rachel is kind of pretty, I guess. I mean, okay, she's very pretty, although, since she

3

is my cousin, I don't really think about her that way. She has blond hair and blue eyes and that kind of very clean, very wholesome look. She's one of those people who always know the right clothes to wear and how to look like they just walked out of one of those fashion magazines girls like. She's also very graceful because she takes gymnastics, even though she says she's too tall to ever be really good at it.

Cassie is sort of the opposite. For one thing, she's usually wearing jeans and a plaid shirt, or something else real casual. She's black and wears her hair very short most of the time. She had it longer for a while, but then she went back to short, which I like. Cassie is quieter than Rachel, more peaceful, like she always understands everything on some different, more mystical level.

I guess you could say I kind of *like* Cassie. Sometimes we sit together on the bus, even though I never know what to say to her.

"You guys going home?" I asked Rachel. "You shouldn't go through the construction site by yourselves. I mean, being girls and all."

That was a mistake. I should never have suggested to Rachel that she's weak or helpless. Rachel may *look* like Little Miss Teen Model or whatever, but she thinks she's Storm from the X-Men.

"Are you going to come and protect us, you big, strong m-a-a-a-n?" she said. "You think we're helpless just because—"

"I'd appreciate it if they did walk with us," Cassie interrupted. "I know *you're* not afraid of anything, Rachel, but I guess I am."

Rachel couldn't say much about that. That's the way Cassie is—she always has the right words to stop any argument without making anyone feel bad.

So, there we were. The five of us—Marco, Tobias, Rachel, Cassie, and me. Five normal mall rats heading home.

Sometimes I think about that one, last moment when we were still just normal kids. It's like it was a million years ago, like it was some totally different group of kids. You know what I was afraid of right then? I was afraid of admitting to Tom that I hadn't made the team. That was as scary as life got back then.

Five minutes later, life got a lot scarier.

To get home from the mall we could either go a long way around, which is the safe way, or we could cut through this abandoned construction site and hope there weren't any ax murderers hanging around there. My mom and dad have sworn to ground me until I'm twenty if they ever find out I've cut through the construction site.

So anyway, we crossed the road and headed into the abandoned construction site. It was a big area, surrounded on two sides by trees, with the highway separating it from the mall. There's a broad, open field between the construction site and the nearest houses. It's a very isolated place.

Originally it was supposed to be this new shopping center. Now it was just all these half-finished buildings looking like a ghost town. There were huge piles of rusted steel beams; pyramids of giant concrete pipes; little mountains of dirt; deep pits that had filled up with black, muddy water; and a creaking, rusted construction crane that I had climbed once while Marco stayed below and told me I was being an idiot.

It was a totally deserted place, full of shadows and sounds that made the hair on the back of your neck stand up. When Marco and I went there during the day, we always found all these beer cans and liquor bottles. Sometimes we found the ashes of little campfires back in the hidden nooks and crannies of the buildings. So we knew that people came there at night. All that was on my mind as we crept through the site.

It was Tobias who saw it first. He had been walking along, gazing up at the sky. I guess he was looking at the stars or something. That's the way Tobias is sometimes—off in his own world.

Suddenly Tobias stopped. He was pointing. Pointing almost straight up. "Look," he said.

"What?" I didn't want to be distracted because I was pretty sure I'd heard the sound of a chain-saw killer creeping up behind us.

"Just look," Tobias said. His voice was strange. Amazed-sounding, but serious at the same time.

So I looked up. And there it was. A brilliant blue-white light that scooted across the sky, going fast at first, too fast for it to be an airplane, then slower and slower. "What is it?"

Tobias shook his head. "I don't know."

I looked at Tobias and he looked back at me. We both knew what we *thought* it was, but we didn't want to say it. Marco and Rachel would have laughed, we figured.

But Cassie just blurted it right out. "It's a flying saucer!"

CHAPTER 2

ᕼ flying saucer?" Marco said. He *did* laugh. That is, until he looked up.

I could feel my heart pounding in my chest. I felt weird and excited and afraid, all at once.

"It's coming this way," Rachel said.

"It's hard to be sure." I could barely whisper, my mouth was so dry.

"No, it's coming this way," Rachel said. She has a very definite way of talking. Like she's totally sure of everything she says.

Rachel was right. Whatever it was, it was coming closer. And it was slowing down. Now I could see pretty clearly what it looked like.

"It's not exactly a flying saucer," I said.

First of all, it wasn't all that big. It was about as long as a school bus. The front end was a pod, shaped almost like an egg. Extending from the back of the pod was a long, narrow shaft. There were two crooked, stubby winglike things, and on the end of each wing was a long tube that glowed bright blue on the back end.

The little spaceship looked almost cute. You know, kind of harmless. Except that it had a sort of tail— a mean-looking tail that curved up and forward, coming to a point that looked as sharp as a needle.

"That tail thing," I said. "It looks like a weapon."

"Definitely," Marco agreed.

The little ship kept coming nearer, going slower all the time.

"It's stopping," Rachel said. She had the same strange, not-quite-real tone in her voice that I had. Like we couldn't believe what we were seeing. Like maybe we didn't want to believe.

"I think it sees us," Marco said. "Should we run? Maybe we should run home and get a camera. Do you know how much money we could get for a video of a real UFO?"

"If we run, they might . . . I don't know, zap us with phasers on full power," I said. I meant it as a joke. Kind of.

"Phasers are only in *Star Trek*," Marco said, rolling his eyes the way he does when he thinks I'm being a dweeb. Like he was some kind of expert on alien spaceships. Right.

The ship stopped and hovered almost directly over our heads, maybe a hundred feet in the air. I could feel the hair on my head standing on end. When I glanced at Rachel it was almost funny. She has this long blond hair and it was sticking straight out in every direction. Only Cassie looked normal.

"What do you think it is?" Marco asked. He sounded a little shakier, not so laid-back now that the thing was so close. To be honest, I was a little scared, too. A *little* scared, as in so terrified I couldn't move. But at the same time, it was all cool beyond any coolness ever. I mean, it was a spaceship! Right there over my head.

Tobias was actually grinning, but that's Tobias for you. He's never scared of weird stuff. It's the normal stuff he can't stand. "I think it's going to land," he said, this huge smile on his face. His eyes were bright and excited, and his blond hair was standing up in clumps.

The ship began to descend. "It's coming right at us!" I cried.

I had to fight an urge to run yammering across the field all the way home, where I could crawl into

10

my bed and pull the covers over my head. But I knew that this was an important, amazing thing. I knew I had to stay and see it all.

I guess the others felt the same way, because we all just stood there, as the ship hummed and glowed and slowly settled down in an open space between piles of junk and tumbled walls. I noticed there were black burn marks along the top of the pod section. Some of the skin of the pod had been melted. It touched the ground and instantly the blue lights went off. Rachel's hair fell back down onto her neck.

"It isn't very big, is it?" Rachel whispered.

"It's about"—I tried to think—"about three or four times as big as our minivan."

"We should tell someone," Marco said. "I mean, this is kind of huge, you know? Spaceships don't just land in the construction site every day. We should call the cops or the army or the president or something. We'd be totally famous. We'd get to be on Letterman for sure."

"Yeah, you're right," I agreed. "We should call someone." But none of us moved. None of us was just going to walk away from a spaceship.

"I wonder if we should try and talk to it," Rachel suggested. She was standing there with her hands on her hips, looking at the spaceship like it was a puzzle she had to figure out. "I mean, we should communicate. If that's even possible."

Tobias nodded. He stepped forward and held out his hands. I guess he was showing whoever was in the ship that he wasn't carrying any kind of weapon or anything. "It's safe," he said in a loud, clear voice. "We won't hurt you."

"Do you think they speak English?" I wondered.

"Well, everyone speaks English in *Star Trek*," Cassie said with a nervous laugh.

Tobias tried again. "Please, come out. We won't hurt you."

<I know.>

I froze. Okay, I had definitely heard someone say "I know," only . . . there hadn't been any sound. I mean, I heard it, but I didn't really hear it.

Maybe this *was* all a dream. I looked kind of sideways at Cassie. She looked back at me. Our eyes met. She had heard it, too. I looked at Rachel. She was turning her head back and forth, like she was looking for where that sound—that wasn't a sound—could have come from. I started to get a sick, twisty feeling in my stomach.

"Did everyone hear that?" Tobias whispered.

We all nodded at once, very slowly.

"Can you come out?" Tobias asked in his loud, talking-to-aliens voice.

<Yes. Do not be frightened.>

"We won't be frightened," Tobias said.

"Speak for yourself," I muttered. The others giggled nervously.

A thin arc of light appeared, a doorway, opening slowly in the smooth side of the pod part of the ship. I stood there, totally hypnotized. I just stared, waiting.

The opening grew, like a crescent moon at first, then a full, bright circle.

And then he appeared.

My first reaction was that someone had fused a person and a deer together. The creature had a head and shoulders and arms that were more or less where they should have been, though the skin was a pale shade of blue. But below that he had fur, a mix of blue and tan, covering a four-legged body that really did look like it belonged to a deer, or maybe a small horse.

He ducked his head out the doorway and I could see that even the fairly normal-looking parts of him weren't all that normal. For a start, he had no mouth, just three vertical slits. And then there were his eyes. Two of them were where they should have been, although they were a glittery green color that was kind of shocking. But the real shock was the *other* eyes. He had what seemed like horns, only on the top of each horn was an eye. The horns could move, twisting to point the eyes front and back or up and down.

I thought the eyes were bad, until I saw the tail. It was like a scorpion's tail, thick and powerful-looking. On the end was a wickedly curved, very sharp-looking horn or stinger. It reminded me of the alien's spaceship. It had seemed kind of cute and harmless, till you noticed the tail. The alien seemed kind of harmless at first glance, too. Then you saw that tail of his and you thought, *Whoa, this guy could do some damage if he wanted.*

"Hello," Tobias said. His voice was gentle, like he was talking to a baby. He was grinning.

I realized I was smiling, too. And at the same moment, I realized that there were tears in my eyes. I can't really describe how it felt, except that it seemed like the alien was someone I'd known forever. Like an old friend I hadn't seen in a long, long time.

<Hello,> the alien said, in that silent way that you only heard inside your head.

"Hi," we all said back.

To my surprise, the alien staggered. He fell out of the ship to the ground. Tobias tried to grab him and hold him up, but the alien slipped from his grasp and fell back to the dirt.

"Look!" Cassie cried. She pointed at a burn that

covered half the alien's right side. "He's hurt."

<Yes. I am dying,> he said.

"Can we help you? We can call an ambulance or something," Marco said.

"We can bandage that wound," Cassie said. "Jake, give me your shirt. We can tear it up and make bandages." Cassie's parents are both veterinarians and she's totally into animals. Not that this was an animal. Not exactly, anyway.

<No. I will die. The wound is fatal.>

"NO!" I cried. "You can't die. You're the first alien ever to come to Earth. You can't die." I don't know why I was so upset. I just knew that way down deep inside, it hurt me to think of him dying.

<I am not the first. There are many, many others.>

"Other aliens? Like you?" Tobias demanded.

The alien shook his big head slowly, side to side. <Not like me.>

Then he cried out in pain, a silent sound that echoed horribly inside my mind. For a moment, I had actually *felt* him dying.

<Not like me,> he repeated. <They are different.>

"Different? How?" I said.

I will remember his answer forever.

He said, <They have come to destroy you.>

15

CHAPTER 3

They have come to destroy you.>

It was strange, the way we all just knew he was telling the truth. No one said "no way" or "you're making it up." We all just knew. He was dying, and he was trying to warn us of something terrible.

<They are called *Yeerks*. They are different from us. Different from you, as well.>

"Are you telling us they're already here on Earth?" Rachel demanded.

<Many are here. Hundreds. Maybe more.>

"Why hasn't anybody noticed them?" Marco said reasonably. "I think someone would have mentioned it at school."

<You do not understand. Yeerks are different. They have no body like yours or mine. They live in the bodies of other species. They are . . .>

I guess he couldn't think of a word to explain Yeerks, so he closed his eyes and seemed to concentrate. Suddenly a bright picture popped into my head. I saw a gray-green, slimy thing like a snail without its shell, only bigger, the size of a rat, maybe. It wasn't a pretty picture.

"I'm guessing that was a Yeerk," Marco said. "Either that or a very big wad of slimy chewing gum."

<They are almost powerless without hosts. They—>

Suddenly we felt that blast of pain, straight from the alien. I could also feel his sadness. He knew his time was almost up.

<The Yeerks are parasites. They must have a host to live in. In this form they are known as Controllers. They enter the brain and are absorbed into it, taking over the host's thoughts and feelings. They try to get the host to accept them voluntarily. It is easier that way. Otherwise the host may be able to resist, at least a little.>

"Are you saying they take over *human beings*?" Rachel asked. "People? These things take over their bodies?"

"Look, this is serious stuff," I said. "You shouldn't be telling us. We're just kids, you know. This is, like, something the government should know about."

<We had hoped to stop them,> the alien continued. <Swarms of their Bug fighters were waiting when our Dome ship came out of Z-Space. We knew of their mother ship and were ready for the Bug fighters, but the Yeerks surprised us—they had hidden a powerful Blade ship in a crater of your moon. We fought, but . . . we lost. They have tracked me here. They will be here soon to eliminate all traces of me and my ship.>

"How can they do that?" Cassie wondered.

The alien seemed to smile with his eyes. <Their Dracon beams will leave nothing behind but a few molecules of this ship, and . . . this body,> he said. <I sent a message to my home world. We Andalites fight the Yeerks wherever they go throughout the universe. My people will send help, but it may take a year, even more, and by then the Yeerks will have control of this planet. After that, there is no hope. You must tell people. You *must* warn your people!>

Another spasm of pain ripped through him, and we all knew he was nearly gone.

"No one is ever going to believe us," Marco said hopelessly. He looked at me and shook his head. "No way."

He was right. If these Yeerks were to wipe out the Andalite's ship, how on Earth would we ever convince people? They'd think we were either nuts or on drugs.

"I don't care if he *thinks* he's going to die, we have to try and help him," Rachel said. "We can get him to a hospital. Or maybe Cassie's parents . . ."

<There is no time. No time,> the Andalite said. Then his eyes brightened. <Perhaps . . .>

"What?"

<Go into my ship. You will see a small blue box, very plain. Bring it to me. Quickly! I have very little time, and the Yeerks will find me soon.>

We all looked at each other. Who was going to be the one to go inside the ship? Somehow we all seemed to agree it would be me. Actually, *I* didn't agree, but everyone else did.

"Go ahead," Tobias said. "I want to stay with him." He knelt beside the Andalite and placed a comforting hand on the alien's narrow shoulder.

I looked at the doorway into the spacecraft. I glanced at Cassie.

"Go ahead," she said, sending me a smile. "You're not scared."

She was wrong; I was plenty scared. But the way she smiled at me, I wasn't about to weasel out.

I walked over to the door of the ship and looked inside. It was surprisingly simple. It looked cozy, almost. Everything was a creamy color with rounded edges and shapes that tended to be oval. That was one of the things that helped me to spot the box so easily. It was sky blue and square, maybe four inches on each side. It seemed kind of heavy for being so small.

I stepped up into the ship. There was no chair, just a sort of open space where I guess the Andalite stood on his four hooves while he worked the few controls. There weren't a lot of buttons or anything. I wondered if the Andalite controlled the ship with his thoughts.

I quickly reached for the box and started to head back outside. But then something caught my eye. It was a small, three-dimensional picture—four Andalites, standing all together, looking like a strange gathering of deer with solemn faces. Two of them looked very small—kids. I realized that this was a picture of the Andalite's family.

It filled me with sadness to think that here he was, dying, a million miles from his family. Dying because he had tried to protect the people of Earth. I felt a small flame of anger against the Yeerks, or Controllers, or whatever they were, for causing this.

I went back to the circle of my friends.

"Here's the box," I told the Andalite.

<Thank you.>

"I, um . . . was that your family? That picture?"

<Yes.>

"I'm real sorry," I said. What else *could* I say?

<There is something I may be able to do to help you fight the Yeerks.>

"What?" Rachel asked.

<I know that you are young. I know that you have no power with which to resist the Controllers. But I may be able to give you some small powers that may help.>

We all looked at each other. All except Tobias, who never took his gaze off the alien.

<If you wish, I can give you powers that no other human being has ever had.>

"Powers?" What was *that* supposed to mean?

<It is a piece of Andalite technology that the Yeerks do not have,> the Andalite explained. <A technology that enables us to pass unnoticed in many parts of the universe — the power to *morph*. We have never shared this power. But your need is great.>

"Morph? Morph how?" Rachel asked, her eyes narrowed.

<To change your bodies,> the Andalite said. <To become any other species. Any animal.>

Marco laughed derisively. "Become animals?" Marco isn't the most accepting person in the world.

<You will only need to touch a creature, to acquire its DNA pattern, and you will be able to *become* that creature. It requires concentration and determination, but, if you are strong, you can do it. There are . . . limitations. Problems. Dangers, even. But there is no time to explain it all . . . no time. You will have to learn for yourselves. But first, do you wish to receive this power?>

"He's kidding, right?" Marco asked me.

"No," Tobias said softly. "He's not kidding."

"This is nuts," Marco said. "This whole thing is nuts. Yeerks and spaceships and slugs taking over people's brains and Andalites and the power to change into animals? Give me a break."

"Yeah, it is beyond weird," I agreed.

"We're off the map of weirdness by this point," Rachel said. "But unless we're all just dreaming, I think we'd better deal with this."

"He's dying," Tobias reminded us.

"*I'll* do it," Cassie said. That surprised me. Cassie isn't usually so quick to decide. But I guess, like Tobias, she *felt* the truth of what the Andalite was saying.

"I think we should *all* decide together," I suggested. "One way or the other."

"What's that?" Rachel asked. She was looking up toward the stars. Far, far overhead, two pinpoints of bright red light were shooting across the sky.

<Yeerks.> The Andalite said the word in our minds, and we could feel his hatred.

CHAPTER 4

Yeerks.>

The twin red lights slowed. They turned in a circle and came back toward us.

<There is no more time. You must decide!>

"We have to do this," Tobias said. "How else can we fight these Controllers?"

"This is so insane!" Marco said. "Insane."

"I'd like more time, but we don't have that choice," Rachel said. "I'm for it."

"What do you say, Jake?" Cassie asked me. It was odd. Like suddenly I was the one who had to decide for everyone?

I looked up at the Yeerk ships. What had the

Andalite called them? Bug fighters? They were circling closer, like dogs sniffing for a scent. I looked down at the Andalite and remembered the picture of his family. Would they even know what had happened to him?

I looked at each of the people around me — my usually funny, occasionally annoying best friend, Marco; Rachel, my smart, pretty, confident cousin; and Cassie, who everyone knew liked animals more than she liked most people.

Finally, I looked at Tobias. It was weird, the feeling I had at that moment, staring at him. A chill or something.

"We have to," Tobias said to me.

Slowly I nodded. "Yes. We have no choice."

<Then each of you, press your hand against one of the sides of the square.>

We did. Five hands, each pressed against one side. Then a sixth hand, different from ours, with too many fingers.

<Do not be afraid,> the Andalite said.

Something like a shock, only pleasurable, seemed to run through me. A tingle that almost made me laugh.

<Go now,> the Andalite said. <Only remember this — never remain in animal form for more than two of your Earth hours. Never! That is the greatest

danger of the morphing! If you stay longer than two hours, you will be trapped, unable to return to human form.>

"Two hours," I repeated.

Suddenly some new fear washed through the Andalite's mind. Linked as I was to him, I could feel it as a dread that crawled up my spine. He was staring up at the sky with his main eyes. Something else was up there with the Bug fighters.

<Visser Three! He comes.>

"What?" I was shaking with this new terror. "What's a Visser? Who's a Visser?"

<Go now. Run! Visser Three is here. He is the most deadly of your enemies. Of all Yeerks, he alone has the power to morph. The same power you now have. Run!>

"No, we'll stay with you," Rachel said firmly. "Maybe we can help."

Again it was as if the alien was smiling at us with his eyes. <No. You must save yourselves. Save yourselves and save your planet! The Yeerks are here.>

We all looked up, craning our necks. Sure enough, the two red lights were sinking toward us. And they had been joined by a third ship, far larger, black as a shadow within a shadow.

"But how are we supposed to fight these . . . these Controllers?" Rachel demanded.

<You must find a way. Now run!>

I jerked from the force of his command. "He's right. Run!" I yelled.

We ran. All but Tobias, who knelt beside the Andalite and took his hand. The Andalite pressed his other hand against Tobias's head. Tobias rocked back, like he'd been shocked. Then he, too, was up and running, stumbling over the loose junk and potholes of the construction site.

A beam of bright red light snapped on. It was a spotlight from one of the Bug fighters. The beam lit up the fallen Andalite and his ship. A spotlight from the second Bug fighter joined the first, and the Andalite shone brilliant as a star.

I hit the dirt hard. I saw my leg lit up within the circle of that spotlight. I yanked it to me and crawled fast, scraping my elbows and knees over sharp stones.

The five of us crouched behind a low, crumbled wall, afraid to move, afraid to look, but just as afraid to look away.

Slowly the Bug fighters descended. It was easy to see where they'd gotten their nickname. They were slightly larger than the Andalite fighter and shaped like legless cockroaches. There were small windows like eyes on the forward-thrust head of the bug. And on either side of the head were two very long, very sharp, serrated spears.

The Yeerk Bug fighters touched down, one on either side of the Andalite ship.

"Okay, you can wake me up now," Marco said in a rattled whisper. "I've had enough of this dream."

The larger ship began to descend. I don't know what it was about that ship, but as it got closer I started to feel like I couldn't breathe. I tried to suck in a deep lungful of air and couldn't. I tried to swallow and couldn't. I wanted to run, but my legs were jelly. I was shaking from a fear so deep it was like nothing I'd ever experienced before. It was the same fear that the Andalite had shown when he'd realized Visser Three was coming.

The ship settled toward the ground. It looked like it was going to land directly on a big rusted earthmover parked there. But as the Visser's ship descended, the earthmover just sizzled and disappeared.

Visser Three's ship was built like some ancient weapon. It reminded me of one of those battle-axes the old-time knights used when they were hacking off the heads of their foes. There was a main part, like the handle of the ax, with a big triangular point on the front. That part had to be the bridge. At the rear were two huge scimitar wings. It was eight or ten times the size of the Bug fighters.

The Blade ship landed. A door opened.

Cassie started to scream. I clamped my hand over her mouth.

They leaped from the ship, whirling and thrusting and slicing the air—creatures that looked like walking weapons. They stood on two bent-back legs and had two very long arms. On each arm there were curved horn-blades growing out of the wrist and elbow. There were other blades at their bent-back knees, and two more blades at the end of their tails. They had feet like a *Tyrannosaurus rex*.

But it was the head that got your attention—a neck like a snake, a mouth that was almost a falcon's beak, and, from the forehead, three daggerlike horns raked forward.

<Hork-Bajir-Controllers.>

I jumped, hearing the Andalite's words in my mind again. They were fainter than before, strained, like someone yelling from far away.

"Did you guys . . . ?" I asked.

Rachel nodded. "Yeah."

<The Hork-Bajir are a good people, despite their fearsome looks,> the Andalite said. <But they have been enslaved by the Yeerks. Each of them now carries a Yeerk in his head. They are to be pitied.>

"Pity. Right," Rachel said grimly. "They're walking killing machines. Look at them!"

But our attention was drawn away by a new form that crept and slithered and shimmied out of the Blade ship.

<Taxxon-Controllers,> the Andalite said. I knew he was trying to tell us all he could, even to the end. Trying to prepare us for what we were up against.

<The Taxxons are evil.>

"Yeah," Marco muttered. "I think I would have guessed that."

They were like massive centipedes, twice as long as a grown man. So big around that if you tried to hug one, your arms wouldn't make it even halfway. Not that anyone would ever want to.

They had dozens of legs that supported the lower two thirds of their bodies. The top third was held upright, and there the rows of legs became smaller, with little lobster-claw hands.

Around the top of their disgusting, tubular bodies were four eyes, each like a wiggling globule of red Jell-O. And at the very end, pointing straight up in the air, was a round mouth, ringed by hundreds of tiny teeth.

Hork-Bajir and Taxxons poured from the Blade ship, spreading out around the area like well-trained marines. They were holding small pistol-sized things that were definitely weapons. They formed a ring around the Andalite and his ship.

Suddenly, one of the Hork-Bajir came straight toward us. He took one big, bounding step and he was practically on top of us.

I hugged the dirt like it was my last hope. I wished I could dig a hole. I saw a flash of Marco's face. His eyes were huge. His lips were drawn back in what could have been a grin, except that I knew it was an expression of pure terror.

CHAPTER 5

The Hork-Bajir pointed his gun, or whatever it was, around at the darkness. His snake head swerved left and right, trying to penetrate the gloom.

<Silence!> the Andalite warned us. <Hork-Bajir do not see well in darkness, but their hearing is very good.>

The Hork-Bajir moved closer still. He was six feet away now, with just the low wall between us. He had to have heard my heart pounding. Maybe he didn't know what the sound was. Maybe he didn't recognize the sounds of five terrified kids whose knees were quivering and teeth were chattering. Kids who were breathing in short, sudden gasps.

I was sure I was going to die, right then. I could see in my mind the way those vicious wrist- and elbow-blades were going to slice my head from my body.

If you've never been really afraid, let me tell you—it does things to you. It takes over your mind and your body. You want to scream. You want to run. You want to wet your pants. You want to throw yourself down on the ground and cry and beg *please, please, please, please don't kill me!*

And if you think you're brave, well, wait till you're cowering a few feet away from a monster who can turn you into coleslaw in about three seconds flat.

But then the Andalite's voice was in my head again. <Courage, my friends.>

And this . . . this warm . . . this . . . I don't have any words to explain it. It was just this warmth that spread all through me. It was like when you're a little kid and you've had a terrible nightmare and you've woken up screaming. You know how you used to feel better when your mom or dad would turn on the light and come in and sit beside you in bed?

That's what it was like.

I mean, I was still terrified. The Hork-Bajir was still there, so real and so deadly. I could hear him breathing. I could smell him. But at the same time, I could feel the panic coming under control. I could feel the strength flowing from the doomed Andalite. He was letting us borrow some of his courage, even though he must have been afraid himself.

The Hork-Bajir moved away. Something new was coming from the Blade ship.

Shaking and chattering, I rose high enough to look over the low wall. Every Hork-Bajir and every Taxxon was turned toward the ship now.

"They're all standing at attention," I whispered.

"How can you tell?" Marco whispered back. "Who knows when a jelly-eyed centipede or a walking SaladShooter from Hell is standing at attention?"

Then *he* appeared.

<Visser Three,> the Andalite said.

Visser Three was an Andalite.

Or at least he was an Andalite-Controller.

"What the . . ." Rachel said. "Isn't that an Andalite?"

<Only once has a Yeerk been able to take an Andalite body,> the Andalite said. <There is only one Andalite-Controller. That one is Visser Three.>

Visser Three walked confidently toward the wounded Andalite. The Visser seemed so much like the Andalite it was hard to tell them apart at first. He had the same mouthless face; the same extra stalk-eyes that turned here and there, checking out everything in all directions; the same powerful yet sleek four-legged body; and the same wicked tail.

But if the Visser *looked* like any normal Andalite, he *felt* different. It was like he was wearing a mask, only you just knew that under the fake sweetness of the mask there was something twisted and foul.

<Well, well,> Visser Three said.

I almost had a heart attack when I realized I was *hearing* the Visser's thoughts.

"Can he hear our thoughts?" Cassie whispered.

"If he can, we're so dead I don't even want to think about it," Rachel told her.

<He cannot hear your thoughts,> the Andalite said. <Unless you are morphed and you direct them to him. You hear his thoughts because he is broadcasting them for all to hear. This is a great victory for him, so he wants all to hear.>

<What have we here? A meddling Andalite?> Visser Three looked more closely at the Andalite's ship. <Ah, but no ordinary Andalite warrior. Prince Elfangor-Sirinial-Shamtul, if I am not mistaken. An honor to meet you again. You're a legend now. How many of our fighters have you shredded? Seven, or was it eight by the time the battle ended?>

The Andalite didn't answer. But I had the feeling maybe it had been more than eight.

<The very last Andalite in this sector of space.

Yes, I'm afraid your Dome ship has been completely destroyed. Completely. I watched it burn as it fell into the atmosphere of this little world.>

<There will be others,> the Andalite prince said.

The Visser took a step closer to the Andalite. <Yes, and when they come it will be too late. This world will be mine. My own contribution to the Yeerk Empire. Our greatest conquest. And then I'll be Visser *One*.>

<What do you want with these humans?> the Andalite asked. <You have your Taxxon allies. You have your Hork-Bajir slaves. And other slaves from other worlds. Why these people?>

<Because there are so many, and they are so weak,> Visser Three sneered. <Billions of bodies! And they have no idea what's happening. With this many hosts we can spread throughout the universe, unstoppable! Billions of us. We'll have to build a thousand new Yeerk pools just to raise Yeerks for half this number of bodies. Face it, Andalite, you have fought well and bravely. But you have lost.>

Visser Three stepped right up to the Andalite. I could feel the Andalite's fear, but rather than cower, he fought the pain of his wound and climbed to his feet. He knew he was going to die. He wanted to die on his feet, looking his enemy in the face.

But Visser Three was not done taunting his foe. <I promise you one thing, Prince Elfangor — when we

have this planet, with its rich harvest of bodies, we will move against the Andalite home world. I will personally hunt down your family. And I will personally oversee the placement of my most faithful lieutenants in their heads. I hope that they will resist, so I can hear their minds scream.>

The Andalite struck!

His tail whipped up and over, so fast you couldn't really see it. The Visser twisted his head aside. The Andalite's tail blade missed the Visser's head by a bare half inch. But it sliced into his shoulder. Blood — or something like blood — sprayed from the wound.

"Yes!" I hissed.

<Aaaaaarrrrrgh!> I could hear the Visser's howl of pain in my head.

At the same time, a blinding beam of blue light shot from the tail of the Andalite ship. It sliced into the nearest Bug fighter. Hork-Bajir and Taxxons scattered.

Even crouching behind the wall, I could feel a wave of blistering heat. The Bug fighter sizzled and disappeared.

<Fire!> Visser Three yelled. <Burn his ship!>

The night exploded in blinding light. Red beams lanced from the Blade ship and the remaining Bug fighter. The Andalite ship glowed, and, with a strange slowness, disintegrated.

Then, in the flash and glow of Dracon beams I saw . . . or *thought* I saw . . . humans. A small group of them, maybe three or four, back in the shadows behind the Visser.

"There are people over there," I told Marco.

"What? Are they prisoners?"

<Take the Andalite,> Visser Three ordered his soldiers. <Hold him for me.>

Three big Hork-Bajir grabbed the Andalite and held him down. Their wrist blades were at his throat, but they knew better than to kill him.

That was to be Visser Three's personal privilege.

Then we saw why a Yeerk as powerful as Visser Three would inhabit the only captured Andalite body. As we watched, Visser Three began to *morph.*

His Andalite head grew large, larger. Much larger. The four horselike legs merged into two and then expanded, each leg becoming as big around as a redwood tree. The delicate Andalite arms sprouted and became tentacles.

"This isn't real," Cassie whispered. "This isn't real."

In the hideously bloated head, a mouth appeared. It was filled with teeth as long as your arm. The mouth grew wider and wider, becoming a monstrous, terrifying grin.

There was nothing left of the Andalite body. A monster had taken its place.

"R-r-r-r-a-a-a-w-w-w-w-g-g-g!" The roar of the beast Visser Three had become made the ground shake.

I covered my ears with my hands.

"R-r-r-r-r-a-a-a-a-g-g-g!"

My teeth rattled from the sound. I heard someone whimpering. It was me.

Visser Three had become a monster that made the Hork-Bajir and the Taxxons look like harmless toys. He reached out with one thick tentacle and grabbed the Andalite by the neck.

"No, no, no," I heard Cassie whispering over and over again. "No, no, no, no."

"Don't look," Rachel said to her. She put her arm around Cassie's shoulder and held her close. Then she reached for Tobias and took his hand. I guess you never really know someone till you see them scared. And even scared to death, with tears running down her face, Rachel had strength to spare.

Visser Three lifted the Andalite straight up in the air, tearing him from the grasp of the Hork-Bajir. The Andalite prince struck again and again with his tail. But each strike was like a pinprick against such a creature.

Visser Three held the Andalite high in the air.

And then Visser Three opened his mouth wide.

CHAPTER 6

I don't know what came over me right then. I had been so afraid. *So* terrified. But it was like something just snapped in my head. I couldn't just hide and watch. I couldn't.

"You filthy—"

I jumped to my feet. I snatched up a piece of rusted iron pipe from the ground and started to climb over that wall.

I guess I just went crazy or something. It had to be craziness, because there was no way that I, alone, armed with a piece of pipe, was going to accomplish anything.

<No!>

The Andalite's silent cry made me hesitate. I felt Marco's hands grabbing at my shirt and pulling me back. Tobias and Marco held me down. Rachel put her hand over my mouth. I was trying to scream, or curse, or something.

"Shut up, you idiot!" Marco hissed. "You're just going to get us all killed."

"Jake, don't." Cassie put her hand on my cheek. "He doesn't want you to die for *him*. Don't you realize? He's dying for *us*."

I shoved Marco and Tobias away angrily. But I was in control of myself again.

I peeked over the wall again. The Andalite prince was helpless in the grasp of Visser Three. I saw him held high in the air. I saw Visser Three open his monstrous, gaping jaws.

I saw the Andalite fall into that open mouth.

The mouth closed. The teeth ripped the Andalite apart. And the Andalite Prince Elfangor-Sirinial-Shamtul died.

At the very end, he cried out. His cry of despair was in our heads. His cry will always be in our heads.

The Hork-Bajir-Controllers began making a huffing sound, like *whuh-whuh-whuh*. Maybe they were laughing or applauding. The Taxxon-Controllers rushed forward and crowded around Visser Three. They seemed to be stretching up toward him, and then I saw why—a piece of the Andalite fell from the Visser's jaws and the nearest Taxxon greedily gobbled it up.

Tobias turned away and covered his face with his hands. Cassie had tears streaming from her eyes. So did I.

I heard a sound that was strange because it was so normal. It was laughter. Human laughter. The humans . . . the Human-*Controllers*—because that's what they were—were laughing, like they were at some kind of a show. For a moment it seemed to me that one of those laughing voices was familiar, like I'd heard it before. But then the sound was swallowed up in the huffing of the Hork-Bajir.

Visser Three morphed out of his monstrous form and slowly regained his Andalite body. <Ah,> I heard him think, <nothing like a good Antarean Bogg morph for . . . taking a bite out of your enemies.>

Again the Human-Controllers laughed and the Hork-Bajir-Controllers huffed, and I heard a familiar human laugh I could not quite place.

Marco started throwing up. It was an understandable thing to do. But somehow that sound caught the attention of the nearest Hork-Bajir.

The snake head turned. He was perfectly still.

We were perfectly still.

The Hork-Bajir turned toward us. The nearsighted eyes were aimed directly at our little hiding place. I don't know who panicked first. Maybe it was me. Maybe we'd just had all the fear and horror we could stand. It was like an electric shock went through all of us. We were running before I had a chance to even know what I was doing.

I ran. I gasped for air.

A cry went up from the Hork-Bajir.

"Split up," I yelled. "They can't follow all of us."

Marco and Tobias and Cassie took off in three different directions. Rachel was still right beside me. Glancing back, I saw the Hork-Bajir hesitate, unsure of who to chase.

Rachel and I are the fastest runners. Tobias is totally out of shape, and Marco and Cassie are too short to be really fast. So I figured if the aliens were going to chase anyone, it ought to be us.

I guess Rachel thought the same thing. She slowed down just a little and began yelling and waving her arms. "Come on, come on, you—" And then she said some words I didn't realize Rachel even knew.

The two nearest Hork-Bajir snapped around and took off after us. "*Ghafrash*! Here! *Ghafrash fit*! Enemy! Get!"

Even in my panic it surprised me. They were talking some mix of their own alien language and ours.

"Ghafrash fit nahar! I get! I kill!"

I ran. Suddenly my foot slammed against something and I was down. I hit the ground hard. The wind was knocked out of me. I tried to fill my lungs again. Rachel ran on. She didn't know I had fallen.

A spear of red light struck a concrete pipe just beside me. The concrete vaporized. The two Hork-Bajir were coming after us, bounding like some devil kangaroos. I was up and running.

Rachel must have realized I wasn't with her anymore. She stopped and started to come back toward me.

"Don't be an idiot!" I yelled. "Run!"

She hesitated just a second. But she knew she couldn't do anything more for me. She ran.

I saw a dark hole ahead and raced toward it.

A doorway. Inside it was as black as a grave. It was one of the buildings that had almost been completed. Just bare concrete walls and scattered junk. But I knew I had been in here before. Marco and I had walked all through it. There were hallways and little side rooms. It was like a maze.

Marco! Rachel! Had they gotten away? And what about Cassie and Tobias?

I tried to get my brain to concentrate as I scurried across the first big room. There was a corridor . . . somewhere. I groped in the dark and found a wall.

I heard the sound of clawlike feet, huge, tearing, rending claw feet scraping over the bare concrete. A bottle went skittering across the floor.

The Hork-Bajir was close! And in the total darkness my superior human vision wasn't much use. But I knew my way around the empty building.

At least, I would have known my way around if my brain had been working.

I felt my hand go into emptiness. A doorway. Yes! It led down a hallway. I went through just as the light came on behind me. Someone had brought a flashlight.

"*Efnud* to tell *fallay nyot fit*? Whatever order."

"No. No need to capture them. Whoever you find, kill."

The first voice had been Hork-Bajir. The second voice was human. And the weird thing was, that voice sounded familiar. I tried to think. I knew I'd heard that voice somewhere. Where? *Where?*

"Just save the head," the human told the Hork-Bajir. "Bring that to me and we can identify it."

I slid quickly along the wall.

The light followed just steps behind me.

I racked my brains. Had there been a passageway . . . ? Yes, there it was. As silently as I could, I slipped into it. The flashlight beam was just inches behind me.

I kicked something soft.

"Hey!"

It was a man! He had been lying on the ground, wrapped in a blanket.

"Hey, get outta here. This is *my* place, and I ain't got nothin' for you to steal."

I started to warn him, but one of the Hork-Bajir was *there*!

The flashlight landed on the homeless man's face. He blinked like an owl.

There was an alcove. Right behind me. I backed through.

The homeless guy screamed. I heard the sound of a scuffle.

Maybe the guy got away. I hope so.

But I never found out, because with the Hork-Bajir distracted, I ran.

I ran and ran and ran. And as I ran, I really hoped it was all just a dream.

CHAPTER 7

Somehow I made it home. I don't know how. I have no memories of anything after that last sight of the Hork-Bajir.

I wish I had no memories of *anything* that happened that night. If only I could forget it all . . .

I called around to the others. Everyone was shaky, but they were all alive. Rachel kept trying to apologize for leaving me. Marco just kept asking me if I was *sure* this wasn't a dream.

I guess I should have had the worst nightmares of my life that night, but I didn't. The world of nightmares was a joke compared to my new reality.

But by the next morning, a Saturday, I half believed it all *had* been a nightmare. The only thing that seemed real . . . really *real* . . . was the way the Andalite had of smiling with just his eyes.

I woke when my mom started pounding on my door.

"Jake, are you awake in there?"

I was now. "Um, yeah," I groaned. "I'm up."

"Your friend Tobias is here."

"Tobias?" What was Tobias doing here?

"It's me." Tobias's voice. "Can I come in?"

"Um, sure." I sat up in my bed and blinked several times, trying to get my eyes unglued. The door opened. I heard Tobias say thank you to my mom.

He was glowing. I swear, he was glowing. Not like he was radioactive or anything, I don't mean that. It's just that his eyes were shining bright, and his face was one big grin, and he seemed to be tingling with energy, bouncing like he couldn't stand still.

"I did it," Tobias said.

I tried to get my hair to go in one direction by raking my fingers through it. "What are you talking about?"

I was yawning when he answered.

"I became Dude."

I stopped yawning. My mouth actually snapped shut. Dude is Tobias's cat. "Huh?"

Tobias glanced around like there might be spies in the room. "I *became* Dude. Just like the Andalite said."

I just stared.

"It was so amazing. It didn't hurt or anything. I was petting him, and thinking about the whole thing last night, right? So I thought, why not give it a try?" He was pacing back and forth, snapping his fingers, bursting with enthusiasm. Very *unlike* Tobias.

"I didn't even know how to begin. So I just made sure the door to my room was locked. Fortunately, my uncle was still asleep."

Tobias has the most screwed-up family I know. He never knew who his father was, and his mom just decided to leave him a few years ago. Since then he'd been shuttled back and forth between his uncle here, and his aunt, who lives on the other coast. His aunt and his uncle can't stand each other, and it's like Tobias is some burden they each try to shove off on the other. I get the feeling neither of them cares about Tobias.

"So there I was, just sitting on my bed, thinking about it. Concentrating. Thinking about becoming Dude. I looked down at my hand." He grinned at me. "What do you think I saw, Jake?"

I shook my head slowly. "I don't know."

"I had fur, Jake. And I was growing claws. You should have seen the *real* Dude. He went nuts. I had to put him outside before I could morph all the way. He clawed me up pretty good."

I swallowed hard. Okay, this was definitely crazy now. "Um, Tobias, is it possible you maybe just dreamed all this?"

"Not a dream," he said. Now he was serious Tobias again. The grin was gone. "It's all true, Jake. All of it."

His eyes met mine. I knew what he was saying. *He* had tried to pretend it was all a nightmare, too. But it was real. I looked away. I didn't want to start believing it had all been real. I wanted it all safely stored away in my head, just another bad dream. Bad dreams should stay in your head, not come jumping out into real life.

"I just kept concentrating on changing," Tobias said, "and in a few minutes, I was . . . not myself anymore."

His eyes bored in on me. "You have no idea what it's like, Jake. Being a cat is so . . . it's . . . I can't even describe it. You're so strong, for one thing. Just all this coiled power, and the way you can move! You know what I did? I jumped onto my dresser. Three feet straight up in the air, and I landed like a feather. Three feet! You know how high that is when you're a cat? It's like a person jumping maybe thirty feet straight up."

He stopped suddenly and looked at me. "You don't believe me, do you?" he said.

"Look, Tobias, it's just that sometimes it's hard to tell the difference between something real and something you're just imagining or dreaming."

"You think I'm crazy."

I considered for a minute. "I don't know, Tobias, let's review the facts. You say you turned into your own pet cat. Turned *into* an actual cat. Yes, I have to say that sounds crazy to me."

Tobias nodded thoughtfully. He gave a little smile. "I understand, Jake. You still don't *want* it to be true."

"What? You mean do I *want* to believe that you can change yourself into a cat? And all the rest of it? Do I *want* to believe that Earth is being invaded by slimy slugs who live in people's brains and turn them into slaves? Do I want to believe that . . . that . . . Duh! No! I don't want to believe any of it."

"And how about the Andalite?" he asked in a quiet voice.

I hesitated. I don't know why, but I didn't want to just pretend the Andalite away.

Tobias put his hand on my arm. "Stand right there."

"What? What are you going to do?"

"I'm going to help you decide whether it's real or not."

"Tobias . . ."

"Just wait. And don't scream or anything."

So I waited.

For a few seconds, nothing happened. Tobias just stood there. I glanced at his face. His eyes . . . his eyes were different. The pupils weren't completely round anymore. I swear there was a reflective greenish light in them. And his mouth was protruding a little, puffing out.

He was shrinking. Growing smaller right before my eyes.

The neck of his shirt was loose. His pants started scrunching up at the ankles. He was shriveling. And at the same time fur—yes, fur!—began to grow on his hands and neck and face. It was gray striped with black, just like Dude's.

I had this absurd desire to start giggling. Tobias was becoming a tabby cat! But I knew if I started giggling I'd just keep on and on and never, ever be able to stop.

Tobias was more cat than human now. The pointed ears rose atop his head. The whiskers stuck straight out from beneath his delicate pink nose. He had dropped to all fours, clothing now half-draped over him, like so many rags. His tail twitched. Yes—his *tail*.

I wondered if I would just drop dead from the lump that had filled my throat, or from the jackhammer pounding of my heart. Then I wondered if I was still asleep.

But if it was a dream, it was a really convincing one.

I was standing there in my bedroom, staring down at a gray-black cat that less than two minutes earlier had been my friend, Tobias.

CHAPTER 8

I hope I'm asleep," I muttered. "I really do."

<You're *not* asleep.>

"Is that you?" I demanded of the cat.

<Can you hear me?> Tobias sounded surprised. Although "sounded" wasn't quite the right word.

"Yes," I said cautiously.

<I did not know I could send thoughts like this,> Tobias said. <Just like the Andalite.>

"I guess it only works when you're . . . morphed."

I am talking to a cat! I realized. And I thought *Tobias* was crazy?

I wondered if Tobias had heard my thought. I concentrated. *Tobias, can you hear me?*

He didn't respond.

"I just thought something at you. Did you hear
me?" I asked.

<No. I don't think it works that way. You have to
be morphed first. Hey, watch this.>

Suddenly Tobias leaped through the air. He
pounced precisely on an autographed baseball that
was lying in the corner. Maybe a four-foot jump.

<That is so excellent! Hey, pull a string for me to
chase.>

"Pull a string? Why?"

<Because it's so fun!>

I dug in my desk drawer and found a length of
string left over from a birthday gift. I'm not exactly
big on keeping my room clean. The string was from
a birthday two years ago.

"How's this?" I drew the string slowly across the
floor, a foot or more from Tobias's nose. He settled
back on his haunches and began wiggling his hind-
quarters. He pounced! He landed on the string,
grabbed it in his sharp teeth, rolled over, and began
ripping at the string like it was the only thing on Earth
that mattered.

I tried pulling the string away, but he pounced
again.

<Yes! Got it!>

"Tobias, what are you doing?"

<Pull it faster! I see it! I got it!>

"Tobias, what are you doing?" I shouted. "You're playing with a string!"

Suddenly he stopped. His tail twitched. He looked up at me with those cold cat eyes, but I'm sure I saw a look of confusion there.

<I . . . I don't know,> he admitted. <It's like . . . like I'm *me*, but I'm also Dude. I want to chase strings, and, oh man, if only there was a real, live mouse around! I'd really love to track it. To follow it so quietly. To listen to its heartbeat. To hear its scratchy little feet. I'd wait till just the right moment, and then a perfect pounce through the air, claws stretched out . . .> He extended his claws to demonstrate.

"Tobias, I think we're learning something here," I said. Amazing, how quickly I was becoming used to the idea of talking to a cat.

<What? What are we learning?>

"I think you aren't *just* Tobias. You really *are* a cat. I mean, you have all the same instincts. You want to do the things a cat wants to do."

<Yes. I can feel it. It's like I'm two different animals melded into one. I can think like a person *and* like a cat.>

"You'd better change back," I said.

He nodded his cat head up and down. Very weird to see, I can tell you—a cat nodding yes in a thoughtful, normal way.

<You're right.>

The change back to human form was at least as strange as the change to cat. The fur disappeared, leaving bare patches of pink skin behind. A nose grew out of the flat cat face. The tail was sucked up like a snake going up a vacuum cleaner.

Tobias stood there, looking embarrassed. He quickly pulled on his clothes. "Maybe with some practice we can figure out how to change back *into* our clothes."

"We?"

He smiled his gentle smile again. "Don't you get it yet, Jake? If *I* can do it, so can you."

I shook my head. "I don't think so, Tobias."

Suddenly he grew angry. He grabbed me by both my shoulders and actually shook me. "Don't you understand, Jake? It's all true. *All* of it."

I pushed him away. I didn't want to hear it.

But he kept after me. "Jake, it's *all* true. The Andalite gave us these powers for a reason."

"Fine," I snapped. "*You* use them."

"I will," he said. "But we'll need you, Jake. You most of all."

"Why me?"

He hesitated. "Geez, Jake, don't you understand? I know what I can do and what I can't do. I can't make plans and tell people what to do. I'm not the leader. You are."

I laughed rudely. "I'm not the leader of anything."

He just looked at me with those deep, troubled eyes — eyes I can now see only in my memory. "Yes, Jake, *you* are our leader. You are the one who can bring us all together and help us defeat the Controllers. We have the ability to be much more than we are, to have the stealth of a cat, and . . . and the eyes of eagles, and the sense of smell of a dog, and . . . and the speed of a horse or a cheetah. We're going to need it all, if we have any hope of holding out against the Controllers."

I wanted it not to be true. I wanted none of it to be true.

But I knew that it was.

I nodded slowly. It felt like I was agreeing to something awful. Like I was volunteering for a trip to the dentist or something much worse. It felt like a million pounds of weight had just landed on my shoulders.

I knew what I had to do next.

"Well," I said grimly. "I guess I'd better go find Homer."

Homer. That's my dog.

CHAPTER 9

It isn't painful. Morphing, I mean.

I petted Homer for a while, feeling like a complete and total fool. "This is the stupidest thing I have ever done," I told Tobias.

"Look, you have to concentrate. At least, I did. I mean, I formed this mental picture of Dude, right? I thought about becoming him."

"I see. So I have to, like, meditate on becoming a dog."

"That's right. You have to think about it. You have to *want* it."

Normally I would have figured he was nuts. But I

had just seen him turn into a cat. So if *he* was nuts, so was I.

I thought about becoming Homer. As I stroked his fur I formed a picture in my mind of me *becoming* Homer. Homer became weirdly quiet while I did it. Like he was asleep, only his eyes were open.

"Just like Dude," Tobias commented. "I think the process kind of puts the animal in a trance or something."

"He's just scared because he thinks his master is a looney tune." I continued stroking Homer's fur and concentrating, and Homer continued to lie very still. "Okay, now what?" I asked Tobias.

"Now we better put Homer outside. He might get slightly freaked by watching you turn into him."

It took Homer about ten seconds to come out of his trance. But then he jumped up, normal, hyperactive Homer again. I put him outside in the yard.

Tobias was sitting patiently when I got back, just waiting. "Give it a try," he urged me. "Think about it. *Want* it."

I took a deep breath. I closed my eyes. I recalled the picture of Homer I'd formed in my mind. I thought about becoming Homer.

I opened my eyes. "Bowwow," I said, laughing. "Guess it didn't work for me, Tobias."

The back of my hand itched and I scratched it.

"Jake?" Tobias said.

"What?"

"Look at your hand."

I looked at my hand. It was covered with orange fur.

I jumped about a foot, straight up in the air. "Ohh! Ohh!" I stared at my hand. The fur had stopped growing.

"Don't be scared," Tobias advised. "Go with it. Now you've stopped the morph. You have to concentrate."

"My hand!" I said. "Fur!"

"Yeah, and your ears . . ." Tobias said.

I ran to the mirror over my dresser. My ears had moved. They had slid up the side of my head, and were definitely larger than they should be.

"Go on, it's so cool!" Tobias said.

"Cool? It's . . . it's . . . creepy. It's weird. It's . . . I mean, look at my hands! I have fur!"

"You have to do this," Tobias said.

"I don't *have* to do anything," I said sullenly.

Tobias nodded. "Okay, you're right. You don't *have* to do this. You can just forget what we saw last night. And forget what we know. And as the Yeerks take over more and more people, you can just ignore it. We can all just go along and grow up in a world where human beings are nothing but bodies to be used by murdering aliens."

Okay, when he put it *that* way it didn't sound like a great option.

"Come on," Tobias urged.

I swallowed hard. I closed my eyes. I thought of Homer. Of *being* Homer.

I felt the itchiness again, and when I opened my eyes, there was fur growing on my arms. And fur growing out of my face. And fur curling up from under my collar. My legs itched and I realized they were growing fur, too.

My bones . . . well, they didn't exactly *hurt*, but they did feel very strange. You know when you go to the dentist and he gives you Novocain so the drill doesn't *really* hurt, but you know it *should* hurt? I guess that's what it's like.

My bones shortened. I could feel my backbone stretching as it extended out into a tail. There was a scraping sound as my hips suddenly folded in. I toppled forward, no longer able to walk upright.

When my hands hit the floor they weren't exactly hands anymore. The fingers were gone. All that was left were short, stubby nails.

My face bulged out. My eyes drew closer together. Tobias got up and tilted the mirror down so I could see myself.

I watched the final transformation as the last patches of my pink human flesh disappeared. And the tail—*my* tail—sprouted to its full length.

I was a dog. It was insane. But just the same. I was a *dog*.

I knew I should be scared by all this, only I wasn't. I was ecstatic. I was giddy. I was thrilled. Happiness just washed over me. Happiness filled me up.

I breathed in through my ridiculously long nose and wow! Wow! The smells. Oh, man, you have no idea! I breathed in and right away I knew my mom was toasting a waffle in the kitchen. And I knew Tobias had walked through the territory of a big male dog. And I knew things I couldn't even explain in human words. It was like being blind all your life and then suddenly you can see.

I ran over to Tobias and sniffed his shoe. I wanted a better idea of who that big male dog was. From the scent of his urine picked up by Tobias's shoe I got a sort of picture of him. See, Homer knew him. His owners called him Streak. He was neutered, like me. He spent most of his time in his yard, but he broke out sometimes by digging under his fence. He got a mix of canned and dry food. Purina. No table scraps, unlike me.

All this information made me happy all over again, and I had to wag my tail. I looked up at Tobias. He looked tall and strange and not very colorful. I wasn't all that interested in *looking* at stuff. Smelling things was way better.

INTRUDER!

There was a noise in the yard. A dog! An unknown dog in MY yard. An INTRUDER!

I ran to the window and perched against it and cut loose.

"Rrrawf! Rrawf rrawf! Rrawfrrawfrrawfrrawf!"

I barked as loud as I could. No WAY some unknown dog was just going to walk through MY yard.

"Jake, get a grip," Tobias said. "That's Homer out there."

Homer? What? But *I* was . . .

I tucked my tail between my legs. What was going on?

"Jake, listen to me," Tobias said. "It's just what happened to me when I morphed into a cat. The dog brain is *part* of your brain now. You have to deal with it."

<But . . . there's a dog in MY yard.>

"That's Homer, Jake. You are Jake. You're just in a body copied from Homer's DNA. That's the *real* Homer out there. You put him out there. Focus. *You* are Jake. Jake."

I took several deep breaths. The smells! Oh, boy, there was this one smell I couldn't quite—

Focus, Jake! I ordered myself. *Focus!*

Slowly I calmed the dog part of my mind.

Let go of the smells. Let go of the sound of a dog out in your yard.

It wasn't easy, that first time. Being a dog is so completely amazing. For one thing, there's nothing halfway about it. You're never *sort of* happy. You're HAPPY! You're never sort of bummed. You're totally, completely bummed. And boy, when you get hungry in dog form, you are nuts on the subject of food.

There was a knock on my bedroom door. Yes, *my* bedroom door. I knew who I was again. I was Jake. Jake with four legs, a tail, and a snout, but Jake.

The knocking seemed incredibly loud to my dog ears.

"Jake, you got Homer in there with you?" My brother Tom's voice. "Mom's on the phone, stop him yapping—"

He opened the door and stepped in. He looked around, confused.

"Who are you?" he demanded of Tobias.

"I'm Tobias. I'm a friend of Jake's."

"Well, where is he?"

"Oh . . . he's around," Tobias said.

Tom looked down at me. There was a strange smell about him. My dog brain couldn't quite identify it. It was an unsettling, dangerous smell. And somehow, in my own mind, I heard the echo of a laugh. A very human laugh I had heard the night before as Visser Three swallowed the Andalite whole.

"Bad dog," Tom said to me. "You keep quiet. *Bad* dog." And then he left.

I was devastated. I wasn't a bad dog. Not really. I was just barking because some other dog was in MY yard. Bad dog? I was a bad dog? No, I wanted to be a *good* dog. I crept into the corner, utterly miserable.

Tobias knelt down and patted my head.

When he scratched me behind the ears, I felt a little better.

CHAPTER 10

I called all the others on the phone after I got done morphing back into my normal body. Tobias took off on his own, saying he'd hook up with us later at Cassie's farm. I was on the kitchen phone with Cassie when Tom came in.

"Oh, there you are," he said.

I covered the mouthpiece. "Yeah. Tobias said you were looking for me before."

"I just wanted you to shut your dog up," Tom said. He turned a chair around backward and straddled it.

I hesitated. For some reason I didn't want to talk to Cassie with Tom listening in. "I'll just see you there in a couple hours, okay?" I told Cassie. I hung up.

I looked over at Tom. He's bigger than me, even though I'm not exactly small. His hair is darker, almost black, while mine is brown.

I had always trusted him. He wasn't like a lot of guys who pound on their younger brother. We were always kind of close. At least, until the last year or so. Somehow we just weren't spending as much time together. Partly it was that he was involved in this club called The Sharing. They did all this stuff together, so he was busy a lot of the time.

The thing is, Tom should have been the very *first* person I told about all the stuff that had happened. But as I was sitting there watching him munch toast, I just had this feeling. This feeling that said *No, this has to be a secret. Even from Tom.*

Instead I told him the other thing I was afraid to tell him.

"I, uh . . . I didn't make the team," I said.

"What team?" he asked. He looked puzzled.

"What team? The basketball team. *Your* old team."

"Oh. Too bad," he said.

"Too bad?" I repeated. I could not believe how little he seemed to care.

"It's just sports," he said. He munched another big bite of toast.

"Just sports?" I couldn't stop repeating what he

said. Tom, saying sports were no big deal? No way. He lived for sports. "Yeah, I guess I just don't have your total skill."

He shrugged. "Well, I quit the team, anyway. A couple days ago."

I practically fell off my chair. "You *quit*? You quit the team? And you didn't even talk to me about it? What's the deal?"

"I didn't say anything because I knew you and Dad would make a big thing of it. Look, there are more important things than throwing balls through hoops," he said. He had this mysterious look in his eyes. I figured he meant girls were the more important thing. "Besides," he added, "we do much cooler stuff at The Sharing. Maybe you should join up."

I was stunned. Obviously, Tom and I were further apart than I had realized.

When we were done talking, I headed outside to mow the lawn. I mow the lawn every Saturday. It's my major chore. That, and taking out the trash, which I hate, because we have to do all this recycling stuff.

When I was finally done mowing and trimming and raking, I hopped on my bike and took off.

I had arranged with everyone to hook up at Cassie's farm. It isn't exactly a normal farm, although it had been in the old days. And they do still have horses and a cow. But now the big red main barn is the Wildlife Rehabilitation Clinic. Cassie's father runs it. They take in any kind of injured animal except pet-type animals. There are always lots of birds, along with squirrels and deer and skunks and so on. Sometimes they get a bobcat or a fox or even a wolf.

Cassie's mom is a vet, too, but she works at The Gardens. That's this huge amusement park that also has a zoo—or I guess they call it a wildlife park. Luckily, Cassie really loves animals. It would have been hard, having her parents, if she *didn't* really love animals.

Me, I have a dog. Tobias has a cat. Cassie has everything from porcupines to polar bears.

By the time I got there, Marco, Tobias, and Rachel were already waiting outside the barn. Rachel had her face turned up to catch the tanning rays of the sun. Cassie wasn't there yet. I figured she was doing chores. She had tons of work to do around there.

"Hey, guys," I said.

Rachel opened her eyes and immediately thrust a newspaper at me. "Look," she said, pointing to an article.

I started to read the article. It wasn't very long. It said that police claimed there had been a disturbance in the construction site the night before. It said several people had called, claiming they'd seen flying saucers landing there, followed by bright lights.

"Cool," I said, looking up. "So the cops know about it now. That's a relief."

"Keep reading," Rachel said.

The article went on to say that the police had arrived on the scene and found a group of teenagers playing with fireworks. The teenagers had run away. Fireworks were discovered at the scene. The police spokesman had laughed at the reports of flying saucers. "It was just a bunch of kids playing where they shouldn't have been," he said. "There were definitely no flying saucers. People shouldn't be so quick to believe nonsense."

"But this is a total lie," I said.

"Ding ding ding ding! Correct answer. Johnny, tell our contestant what he's won," Marco said.

"Did you see the last part?" Rachel pressed.

I read the last sentence. It froze me up good, I can tell you. Police were offering a reward for information on the teenagers.

"They're looking for *us*," Marco said.

"Why would the police be . . . I mean, why would they lie?" I wondered aloud. But the answer was pretty obvious.

Marco laughed his sardonic laugh. "Let's see, Captain Brilliant — would it be because the cops *are* Controllers?"

"Probably not *all* the cops," Tobias pointed out.

71

"If the police have been infiltrated by the Controllers, who knows how many others have, too?" Rachel asked. "Teachers? People in the government? The newspapers and the TV?"

"Math teachers, for sure," Marco joked.

We all looked around nervously, like we expected to find ourselves surrounded by Controllers.

"I tried to tell myself it was all a dream," Rachel said.

"Been there," I said.

For a while no one said anything. We all felt the same terrible feeling — like we were all alone. Like suddenly we were dealing with stuff that was way, way, *way* over our heads.

Marco spoke first. "Look, why do we have to deal with this? I say we just forget it. We never talk about it. We never *morph*. We just deal with our own lives."

Tobias and Rachel both looked at me. They were waiting for me to argue with Marco.

"Marco, I halfway agree with you —" I started to say.

Suddenly Marco just went ballistic. "We could get killed!" he yelled. "Don't you get it? You saw what happened to the Andalite. I mean, this is perilous stuff, Jake. This is for real. Real! We could all get killed."

Tobias was looking at Marco with this sideways look, like he thought maybe Marco was some kind of coward. I knew better. Marco had his reasons.

Marco shook his head. In a quiet voice he said, "Look, I think these Controllers are jerks. But if something happened to me . . . my dad. He wouldn't be able to handle it."

Two years ago, Marco's mom died. She drowned. They never even found her body. Marco's dad lost it big-time. He totally fell apart. He quit his job as an industrial engineer because he couldn't handle being around other people. Now he was working as a night janitor, making barely enough to support Marco. He spent his days sleeping or watching TV with the sound off.

"You can all think I'm a weasel if you want," Marco said. "I don't care. But if I get killed or something, my dad will flat-out die. He's only hanging in there because of me."

I wondered if I should go pat him on the back or something. But if I had, Marco, being Marco, would have just said something sarcastic.

"There's Cassie," Rachel said, shielding her eyes and looking off across the open field.

A horse, galloping across the green. Its black mane was flying in the warm breeze. I didn't see any rider.

The horse slowed, trotting closer, and suddenly I had a strange feeling about the horse.

"Cassie and I have been here for a while," Rachel said by way of explanation. "She's really good at this. Look how fast she can do it."

The horse nickered softly. Then the animal began to melt. The big brown eyes became slightly smaller. The long muzzle became a human mouth.

A thing that was part horse and part Cassie smiled at us with big horse teeth and said, "Hey, kids."

Marco suddenly sat down. Very hard. He had never seen a morphing.

"It's cool," I said, trying to sound very relaxed. "It's just Cassie."

I decided I'd better be a gentleman and look away. After all, when Tobias and I had morphed, we'd kind of morphed right out of our clothes. But I noticed that as Cassie emerged from the horse, she was wearing a skintight blue outfit. One of those outfits girls wear to the gym.

I watched and saw something beautiful happen. For just a few seconds, she stayed half horse and half human. She reminded me of the Andalite. I realized it was deliberate. Cassie was controlling the way she morphed.

"Jeez, Rachel," I said. "You're right. Cassie is good."

Suddenly we heard the sound of tires on gravel.

We all spun around. Down the gravel and dirt road came a single black-and-white car.

"The cops!" Tobias cried.

CHAPTER 11

Cassie. Morph. Now!" I snapped. The police car was coming fast. "We do *not* want to have to explain a half horse half person."

"Which way should I morph?" Cassie wailed. "Horse or human?" She reared up slightly on her hind legs.

I knew what was happening. She was fighting the horse's urge to panic.

"Human, human, human!" I said. "Everybody, stand in front of her!"

The police car squealed to a stop, sending the gravel flying. A single policeman stepped out.

I waved at him.

"Morning," he said. "You kids, uh . . . hiding something?"

I wanted to look over my shoulder and see what kind of shape Cassie was in. But that would have been a mistake. "Hiding something?" I repeated.

"Step aside, all of you," he ordered.

We did, revealing Cassie. Fully human.

The policeman looked puzzled. But then he shrugged.

I breathed a huge sigh of relief.

"Can we help you, officer?" Rachel asked in her best "responsible" voice.

"We're making some inquiries," he said, still looking at Cassie like something must be wrong with her. "We're looking for some kids who were shooting off fireworks in the construction site across from the mall last night."

Suddenly Marco started coughing.

"Something the matter with him?" the policeman asked.

"Nope," I said. "Nothing wrong with him."

"We want these kids," the policeman said. "We want them real bad. See, it was dangerous what they did. Could have been someone hurt. So we want to find the kids."

Suddenly I knew. He was one of *them*. The policeman was a Controller. I looked at his face. It seemed normal. But inside his head was a creature from another planet—an evil, parasitic slug. Just behind those normal, human-looking eyes, something vile lurked.

"I don't know anything about it," I lied.

He looked at me real close, and I began to sweat.

"Hey, you know what?" he said. "You look familiar. You look like a young man I know named Tom."

"He's my brother," I said. I was trying not to let my voice go weird. But I just couldn't forget the fact that it wasn't really some normal, human cop I was talking to. It was a Yeerk. This wasn't even a human anymore. Not really. It was a Human-Controller. The human brain was totally enslaved.

"Tom's your brother, eh? Well, he's a good kid. I know him from The Sharing. I'm one of the adult supervisors. Great group, The Sharing. You should come to a meeting."

"Yeah, um, Tom invited me already," I said.

"We have a lot of fun."

"Yeah," I repeated.

"Well, you call me if you hear anything about these kids in the construction site. I should warn you—they may come up with some wild story to conceal their guilt. But you're too smart to believe a bunch of crazy lies, aren't you?"

"He's a regular genius," Marco said.

Finally the policeman took off.

"Okay, rule number one," Rachel announced. "We don't do anything to attract attention. We have to be secret about *everything*. Especially morphing."

Cassie looked embarrassed. "Yeah, it was stupid of me. It's just, man! It is so amazing, running like that. Out in the open spaces, running and running."

"How did you manage to morph with *clothing*?" I asked. "When Tobias and I did it . . . well, let's just say it's a good thing neither of you girls was around."

"It took some practice," Cassie said. "And it can only be tight clothing. I tried it with a coat on. It got shredded. I don't know what we'll do in the winter."

"That's not going to be a problem," Marco said firmly. "Because there isn't going to be any more morphing."

"Maybe Marco is right," Rachel said. "This is too big for us. We're just kids. We need to find someone important to tell this to. Someone we can trust."

"We can't trust anyone," Tobias said flatly. "Anyone could be a Controller. We tell the wrong person, we are all dead. And the whole world will be doomed."

"I don't want to stop morphing," Cassie said. "Do you realize all we could do with this power? We could communicate with animals, maybe. Help save endangered species."

"Humans may be the next endangered species, Cassie," Tobias said quietly.

"What do you say, Jake?" Cassie asked.

"Me?" I shrugged. "I don't know. Marco's right, we could all get killed. Rachel's right, this is too major for a bunch of kids." I hesitated. I didn't like what I was about to say. "But Tobias is right, too. I mean, the whole world is in danger. And we can't trust anyone."

"So, what do we *do*?" Rachel demanded.

"Hey, it's not up to *me* to decide," I said hotly.

"Let's take a vote," Rachel said.

"I vote we try to live long enough to get driver's licenses," Marco said.

"I vote we do what the Andalite said — fight," Tobias said.

"You've never even been in a fight," Marco sneered. "You can't handle the bullies at school. Suddenly now you want to kick butt on that Visser Three monster?"

Tobias said nothing, but a blush spread up his neck.

"I vote with Tobias," Rachel said, giving Marco a dirty look. "I wish we could dump all this on someone else. But we can't."

"Let's think it over for a while," Cassie said. "This is a big decision. I mean, it's not like we're deciding whether to wear jeans or a skirt."

I was relieved. Thank goodness for Cassie.

"Yeah, let's wait for a while," I agreed. "In the meantime, no one say anything to anyone. We just go back to normal life."

There was a smirk on Marco's face. He thought he'd won. But I wasn't so sure. Tobias was still blushing. He sent a secret, grateful look to Rachel.

Marco and I took off toward my house again, trying to act normal. We talked about the baseball season. We talked about who was going to slaughter who in Dead Zone 5, which is this game we were going to play at my place.

By the time we'd reached my house, we'd run out of stuff to talk about.

We played Dead Zone for a while. Neither of us did very well. Face it, games just weren't all that interesting anymore. My mind was totally not there.

Tom came in after a while. "Hey, you guys," he said. "Can I give that a try?"

It had been months since Tom had done anything with me like play a game.

"Sure." Marco moved over and gave Tom his control stick.

We played for a few minutes, and Tom did pretty

well. But then it was like he got bored or something. He gave the control back to Marco and just sat back and watched.

"You guys hear about all the stuff going on with the construction site last night?" he asked me.

Marco jerked in surprise.

"What stuff?" I said.

"It was in the newspaper," Tom said casually. "They said some kids were there shooting off fireworks. A bunch of morons who live around there decided it was flying saucers or something." He laughed. "Flying saucers, right."

Marco and I both laughed, too.

"Yeah. And it was just these kids playing with fireworks," Tom said.

"Uh-huh," I said. I was trying very hard to concentrate on the game.

"You were out at the mall last night, weren't you?" Tom asked me.

"Uh-huh."

"Did you come back through the construction site?"

I shook my head. "No way."

"Didn't see any kids hanging around there, maybe?"

"Nope."

"It's not like I'd get them in trouble," Tom said.

"I mean, I think it's kind of cool. They're just shooting off fireworks and they get all these people terrified of flying saucers."

"Uh-huh."

"Flying saucers," he said. He laughed again. "Only complete dips believe that kind of stuff." He leaned close. "You don't believe in that, do you? Aliens and spaceships and little green men from Mars?"

I wanted to say no, none of them had been little or green. But I just said, "No way."

Tom nodded and stood up. "Cool. You know, Jake, I feel like we haven't been hanging around much lately."

"I guess not," I agreed.

"That's too bad," he said. He snapped his fingers like he'd just had an idea. "You know, you should join The Sharing. Marco, too."

"Why should we join?" Marco asked.

Tom just grinned. "I gotta go," he said. He gave me a playful punch on the shoulder. "See you guys later. And don't forget—let me know if you hear anything about those kids at the construction site."

He left.

Marco looked at me. "Jake. He's one of them."

"What?"

"Tom. Tom is one of *them*. Your brother is a Controller."

CHAPTER 12

I swung my fist and caught Marco in the side of the head.

He jumped back and I swung again. But Marco was quick. He dodged my second swing, and I slipped and went down.

Marco snatched the bedspread off my bed, threw it over me to tangle up my arms, and sat on me.

"Jake, quit acting like a stupid jerk," he said.

I was trying to grab him, but he had me pretty good. "Take that back!" I yelled.

"Not likely," Marco said. "You think it's just a coincidence he's suddenly all interested in what happened at the construction site?"

I knew it looked bad. Even while I was struggling to get free and kick Marco's butt. I had this sudden flash about the smell I'd noticed on Tom when I was morphed into a dog. And there was that laugh I'd heard at the site.

But no. No! This was Tom, my big brother. Tom would never, ever have let those slimy creeps into his head. Never.

"I'll let you up if you'll calm down," Marco said. "Look, maybe I'm wrong, okay?"

I stopped struggling, and Marco let me up.

"You have to admit, Jake, it doesn't look good."

"Tom is *not* one of them, *okay*? That's final," I said.

"Whatever," Marco said. "Just don't punch me again, 'cause I might have to hit you back."

Just then I heard this fluttering noise at my window. Like someone beating on it very softly. I went to the window, followed by Marco.

There was a bird there. Some kind of huge bird, like an eagle or a hawk, beating its wings against the window.

<Let me in, all right? I can't hover here forever!>

Marco's eyes went wide. He'd heard it, too.

I opened the window and the bird flew straight in. It landed on my dresser. It was almost two feet long, mostly brown, with gnarled talons and a sharp, hooked beak.

"It's some kind of eagle or something," Marco said.

<A red-tailed hawk, actually,> Tobias said.

"Is that you, Tobias?" Marco demanded. "I thought we weren't going to do any more of this morphing."

<I never agreed to that.>

"Well, morph back, Tobias," I said. "You know what the Andalite said—never stay in any form for more than two hours."

Tobias hesitated. He tilted his hawk's head and peered at me with an incredibly concentrated gaze. At last, he hopped over onto my bed.

Let me tell you something, it is beyond weird, watching feathers turn into skin. The brown feathers ran together and merged and turned pink. It was like the feathers were melting. Like they had turned into wax and were being heated up.

The beak disappeared quickly, and lips grew out of it. The talons split into five and became toes.

Halfway through the process of changing, Tobias was a lump, half-pink, half-brown, with featherlike patterns still visible on his back and chest. His face was small and mostly human, except that he still had those sharp, alert hawk's eyes. Two tiny, shriveled arms protruded from the front of his chest with fingers like a baby's.

All in all, it was a pretty disgusting sight.

But the human DNA asserted itself over the hawk's and he became more normal. About three minutes after he'd started the change, there was a completely normal Tobias, sitting naked on the end of my bed.

"I haven't figured out how to morph clothes yet, like Cassie," he said sheepishly. "Can I borrow some?"

I loaned him a pair of pants and a shirt, but my shoes were all the wrong size.

"That was the coolest thing I've ever done in my life," Tobias said. His whole face was glowing. "I was riding the thermals."

"What's a thermal?" I asked.

"That's when there's warm air rising up from the ground. It forms this cushion under your wings. You can just float up there. Like a mile up! You just surf the thermals. You guys have got to do it! It is the best thing ever."

"Tobias, how on Earth did you do a hawk morph?" I asked.

"There's an injured hawk right there in Cassie's barn," he said. "There's this cool osprey, too, but I decided on the hawk."

"How did you fly if the hawk you morphed from was injured?" I wondered.

Marco shook his head pityingly. "Jake, do you pay *any* attention in biology class? DNA has nothing to do with some injury. The DNA wasn't broken, just a wing."

I ignored Marco. "You're lucky Cassie's dad didn't catch you," I said to Tobias.

"He's so depressed," Tobias commented.

"Who's depressed? Cassie's dad?"

"No, the hawk. I mean, I think he knows they aren't trying to hurt him or anything, but he can't stand being cooped up there while his wing heals." Tobias's eyes darkened. "It's terrible when birds have to be locked up in cages. They should be free."

"Yeah, free the birds," Marco commented sarcastically. "I'll get the bumper stickers printed up."

"You wouldn't have that attitude if you'd been up there with me," Tobias said angrily. "It was cool being a cat and all. But a hawk! It's just total, absolute freedom."

I hadn't ever seen Tobias so happy. I mean, Tobias has a pretty lousy home life. Thinking about it, I suddenly had this feeling. . . .

I repeated the warning. "No more than two hours

in any morph, right? You keep track of the time, right?"

Tobias smiled. "Yeah. I don't have a watch or anything, but with hawk eyes you can actually see the hands of someone's watch when they're half a mile below you. It's like being Superman. You can fly, plus you have super vision."

"Now he's Superman," Marco muttered.

"I was looking around. I guess I thought I might be able to see something from the air," Tobias said. "I was looking for something that might be a Yeerk pool."

The phrase sounded vaguely familiar. I remembered Visser Three saying something about "Yeerk pools." "What's a Yeerk pool?" I asked Tobias.

"It's where the Yeerks live in their natural state. Every three days a Yeerk has to leave his host body and go into the Yeerk pool to soak up nutrients. Especially Kandrona rays."

Marco and I exchanged a suspicious look. Neither of us knew any of this.

"At the end," Tobias explained, "when the Andalite told us all to run for it, I stayed behind for a few seconds. I guess maybe I was too scared even to run."

I shook my head. I knew better. Tobias just hadn't

wanted to leave the Andalite alone. I think maybe the Andalite meant even more to Tobias than to the rest of us.

"Anyway, he gave me . . . visions, I guess you'd call them. Pictures. Information. A lot of it, all at once. All jumbled. I haven't even started to sort it all out. But I do know about the Yeerk pools and the Kandrona."

Marco held up his hand, silencing Tobias. "Let me check the door," he said. He went to my door and peeked out into the hallway. "All clear," he announced.

Tobias gave Marco a questioning look.

"Tom," Marco said. "He's one of them."

"Don't make me hurt you," I warned him angrily. "Tom is not a Controller."

"Either way, we should be careful," Tobias said. He lowered his voice. "The Kandrona is a device that produces Kandrona particles. See, it's like this little portable version of the Yeerk's own home sun. The Yeerks need Kandrona particles to live, like a human needs vitamins or whatever. The Kandrona particles are beamed from wherever the Kandrona is and concentrated in the Yeerk pool. Once every three days, every Yeerk has to leave his host and go into the pool. They soak up the particles and then they reenter the host body."

"What does this have to do with you flying around playing Superman?" I asked.

"Well, it seems dumb now, but I was thinking maybe I could see the Yeerk pool." He made a rueful smile. "Saw a lot of swimming pools and some ponds. You get up there and you realize there are ponds and lakes and streams everywhere. But I didn't see anything special."

"And what if you found some Yeerk pool? Then what?" Marco demanded.

"Then we'd blow it up," Tobias said.

"Wrong," Marco said. "We decided *not* to get into this."

"No, we decided not to decide yet," I said.

"Well, I've decided," Tobias said.

"Suddenly the wimp is a hero," Marco sneered.

This time Tobias didn't blush. "Maybe I just found something worth fighting for, Marco."

"You don't even fight for yourself," Marco said.

"That was before," Tobias said softly. "Before the Andalite. Before he died trying to save us. I can't let that go. I can't let him die for nothing. So whatever you guys decide, I'm going to fight."

CHAPTER 13

We find the Yeerk pool," Tobias said. "And when we do, we blow it up and kill every one of those evil slugs."

I expected Marco to start yelling. But Marco is pretty smart. He could tell that Tobias had reached me with his talk about the Andalite. So he just smiled, a little sneakily.

"Remember that cop today, the one who is so interested in finding whoever was at the construction site? The cop who is probably a Controller?"

"What about him?" I said.

"Well, let's see. He invites you to join The Sharing. And now along comes Tom. And suddenly he is very interested in whatever happened at the construction site. And guess what? Tom also invites you to join The Sharing."

Tobias nodded in agreement. "Maybe this Sharing is an organization for Controllers."

Marco smiled. He's my best friend and all, but sometimes Marco really makes me mad.

"We're pretty sure the cop is a Controller. And I don't care what you say, Jake, I think Tom is, too. So, here's the deal. You want to get into this fight against the Yeerks?" Marco asked me. "Fine. Let's see how much you want to do it when it turns out it's your own brother you have to destroy."

That stopped me cold.

"It's not exactly some video game, is it?" Marco said. "This is reality. You don't know anything about reality, Jake. Nothing bad has ever really happened to you. You have this perfect family. Like I *used* to have."

His voice cracked a little. He never talked about his mom's death.

I realized he was right. I didn't know about reality. Not the way reality had happened to Marco — and to Tobias.

"So maybe we just walk away from this," Marco said. "Let someone else fight this fight. Sorry about the Andalite, but I've got enough death in my family."

"No," I said, surprising myself. "The Andalite gave us the morphing power for a reason. It wasn't just for the fun of being a dog or a horse or a bird. He hoped we would fight."

"Then maybe Tom is the enemy," Marco said. "Maybe it's your own brother you'll end up destroying."

"Yes," I said. My throat felt all tight. "Maybe that's what will happen. Maybe not. But the first step is to find out more. And I think maybe the way to do that is to check out this meeting of The Sharing. Tonight. I'll call the others. Anyone wants to come, cool. You want to stay out of it, Marco, that's cool, too."

He hesitated. He sent Tobias an angry look. But he said, "Okay, it's just a meeting, right? We go and see. I'm in for that."

I called the others. Rachel agreed quickly. Cassie had to think about it for a little while, but she agreed, too.

I told Tom we were interested in attending the meeting. Me and Marco and Rachel and Cassie. We'd already decided Tobias would be there, too. Only in a different way.

"Tonight's a great meeting to come to," Tom said enthusiastically. "We're having a bonfire on the beach.

You know, hanging out, playing games and stuff. We play night volleyball, which is so funny because half the time guys can't even see the ball. It's great. It's the best organization. You'll love it."

Listening to him, it sure didn't *sound* like The Sharing was connected with the Yeerks. You couldn't really picture Visser Three or a bunch of Taxxons playing volleyball.

I was thinking maybe we were all just nuts. The Sharing was probably just like some new kind of coed Boy Scouts or something.

It wasn't that far to the beach, so we decided not to drive there with Tom. We walked. Tobias walked partway with us, then he stepped behind a dark dune as we got close to the shore. A few minutes later we saw a hawk take flight. There aren't many thermals at night, so he had to work to get altitude. But then I guess he found a decent enough updraft, because he soared up and away till he disappeared.

"I have got to try that," Cassie said. "It looks wonderful."

"Yeah," I agreed. Ahead, the bonfire burned bright on the dark beach. People were all around it, playing, talking, eating. Kids from school. Adults. People I didn't know. Others I did.

Were they all Controllers? I wondered. How could I ever know? And was my own brother one of them?

After about an hour of hanging out there on the beach, I was sure I was nuts. There was no way these guys were aliens. We played some volleyball, me and Tom together on one team. We ate the barbecue ribs they had. I mean, it was just like this normal, good time.

The sand was still warm. The night air was chilly, but near the fire it was nice.

"Now you see why I enjoy this?" Tom asked me.

"It's cool," I said. I looked around at all the people having fun. "I didn't realize it was so much fun."

"Well, that's not *all* it is," Tom said. "I mean, it's more than just fun. The Sharing can do all kinds of things for you. Once you're a full member."

"How do you get to be a full member?" I asked.

He smiled mysteriously. "Oh, that will come later. First you become an associate member. Later the leaders will decide whether to ask you to become a full member. Once you become a full member . . . the whole world changes."

At that moment, something weird happened. I was looking at Tom, and he was smiling at me. But then his face kind of twitched. His head started to pull to one side, like he was trying to shake his head only he couldn't quite do it. For just a split second there was a look in his eyes—scared or . . . or something.

He was looking right at me, and it was like some different person, some scared person, was looking out of those same eyes.

Then he was back to normal. Or what looked like normal.

"I have to go for a while now," he said. "The full members have a separate meeting. You guys stay here and have fun. Have some more of that barbecue. It's great, isn't it?"

With that, he was gone into the night.

I felt like I had swallowed barbed wire.

Marco and Cassie came over. They had just finished playing Frisbee in the surf with some other kids. Marco was laughing.

"Okay," he said, "I admit it. I was wrong. These are just normal people having a good time. And Tom is not a Controller."

I didn't know whether to laugh or cry. Marco was wrong.

I knew what I had seen in Tom's eyes—he was trying to warn me. Somehow he had managed to gain control of his face for just a second before the Yeerk in his head had crushed him.

Tom—the *real* Tom, not the Yeerk slug in his brain—had tried to warn me.

CHAPTER 14

They're all going off to a separate meeting," I said. "All the *full* members. I'd sure like to know what goes on in that meeting." I struggled to sound normal, but my insides were churning.

"I saw people heading that way." Rachel pointed.

"Let's see if we can get close," I said.

"What's going on?" Marco asked. "I thought we just decided everything was normal here."

It was Cassie who answered him. "Nothing is normal here," she said. "Can't you feel it?" She shivered. "All these so-called *full* members, they're all being so perfectly nice. So perfectly helpful. They're so perfectly normal it's abnormal. And all the time their eyes are following you, watching you. Watching you like . . . like a hungry dog watching a bone."

"Creepy," Rachel agreed. "Like if you took cheerleaders, combined them with gym teachers, and made them all drink ten cups of coffee."

"They are all just a little too happy, aren't they?" Marco admitted. "People keep telling me how all their problems disappeared once they became a full member of The Sharing. It's like some cult or something."

"I'm getting into that secret meeting," I said. I had to *know*. I had to be dead sure. "Let's get away from the fire. Over behind that lifeguard stand."

"How are you going to get into the meeting?" Marco asked.

"They won't worry about some stray dog that's walking along the beach," I said.

"Some stray . . . oh," Marco said.

"Good idea," Cassie said. "I'd do it, too, but the only morph I can do is a horse. They would notice a horse."

I checked to see that no one could see us. I waved over my head. A few seconds later, Tobias came swooping silently out of the starlit sky. He landed on the lifeguard stand.

<What's up?>

"The full members are off in some private get-together," I told him. "Do you know where they are?"

<Of course. With these eyes I can see the mice scampering through the dune grass. Nice, plump, tasty-looking things.>

"Tobias! Get a grip. Don't start eating mice just because you're in a hawk's body. What's next? Roadkill?"

He didn't say anything. Maybe he was offended at my suggestion that he would ever eat roadkill. Or, worse, maybe he *wasn't* offended.

"Where are the full members?" I asked.

<About a hundred yards down the beach. There's a little bowl-like area formed by the dunes. There are people posted all around, though, like guards.>

I nodded. "Good job. Tobias, you've been in that body for more than an hour. You need to morph back."

<No, I'll keep watch from above for a while longer,> he said.

"No, Tobias," I said sharply. "You need to morph back. You've done what we needed you to do."

<Um, there is that little problem . . . I don't exactly have any clothes on.>

"Marco has your clothes in a bag. Rachel and Cassie will turn away while you morph."

Cassie grinned. "I am going to have to teach you boys how to morph clothing."

Still Tobias hesitated. <I hate changing back. It's like going back into a prison or something. I hate it when I don't have wings.>

"Tobias, you can always return to your hawk morph later," Rachel reassured him. "Now, come on, both of you. I'll look the other way so your delicate boy modesty isn't offended."

I took a deep breath. It was only my second morph. It still seemed totally ridiculous that I was even thinking about *becoming* a dog. But as I concentrated, I could begin to feel the itchiness and the squirmy feeling as Homer's DNA combined with the Andalite's technology and began to change me.

At the same time, I could see fingers growing from the ends of Tobias's wings.

"Keep a grip on your human side," Cassie warned me. "We can't have you off chasing cats or whatever. You need to focus hard on staying in control."

I started to say, "Yes, I know," but it came out "Rowr, rowwr, ruff!" I was already too changed to make normal human speech.

I thought my answer instead. <Yes, I know, Cassie. Don't worry.>

"But I *do* worry," she said softly.

I nuzzled her hand with my cold nose and she patted my head. I set off across the sand.

Cassie had been right to warn me. The dunes, the surf, the low chirping of seabirds in their hidden nests—all of it was so perfect for distracting my dog mind.

I heard something breathing in the sea grass, and then it broke and ran! I was off after it before I could even think. It ran and I chased. I think it may have been a chipmunk or something. I never could be sure, because it found a hole and went diving in.

I dug frantically in the sand for a while before my human brain realized, *Whoa, Jake, this is not what you're supposed to be doing. Stop it!*

I made myself walk toward the meeting. I could hear the murmur of voices. I started to creep closer, then I realized that was dumb. Dogs don't creep around. They just walk or run. If I went around acting like "spy dog," *that* would make people pay attention.

So I wandered along, like any dog out for an evening stroll along the beach. My tongue lolled out of my mouth. My tail wagged occasionally. The only thing I had to be careful of was not to let Tom see me too clearly. After all, I looked exactly like Homer.

Basically, I *was* Homer.

I approached the edge of the area. There were high dunes all around. About twenty or thirty people were standing together. Unfortunately, with my weak dog eyes I couldn't see them very well in the darkness.

But I could hear them. I could hear them amazingly well. Sounds that I would barely have noticed with my human hearing were as loud as a stereo set on nine.

And I could smell. It's funny about smell. As a human you don't really get into it. But when I lay back and let my dog abilities come up, smell became as good as sight. Different, but just as good for some things.

I heard Tom's voice. And I smelled a subtle combination of things that meant he was not too far away.

There was a man on guard, but all he did was look down at me, then look away. No one cares about a stray dog.

I was beginning to realize why the Andalite had given us the power to morph. There are things you can do as an animal that you could never do as a human.

The members all seemed to be waiting for someone to arrive. I heard Tom say, "He should be here soon. Wait, here he comes."

There was a stirring, muttering sound. I heard footsteps approach. I moved closer but stayed out of the light.

"Everyone, quiet. We have problems," the voice said.

The voice! I knew that voice. It was the same voice that had been at that construction site. It was the voice that had said, "Just save the head. Bring that to me, and we can identify it."

I crept a little closer. I had to look hard to see him with my dog sight. But then, when he turned just the right way, I saw him. I recognized him. It was someone I knew. Someone I saw every day at school.

None other than Assistant Principal Chapman.

My assistant principal was a Controller.

"Item one. We still have not found the brats who were at the construction site," Chapman said. His voice was hard. "I want them found. Visser Three wants them found. Does anyone have any clues?"

For a moment no one spoke. Then I heard a second familiar voice.

"It could have been anyone," Tom said. "But it *might* be the one who's my brother, Jake. I know he goes through the construction site sometimes. That's why I brought him here tonight. So we could either make him ours . . . or kill him."

CHAPTER 15

Either make him ours . . . or kill him."

I felt like someone had punched me.

I told myself that Tom was a Human-Controller. Some slimy, snotty slug from another planet was in his brain controlling him. When he talked to me it wasn't even Tom, not really. It was a Yeerk.

My brother . . . one of *them*. Chapman . . . one of *them*.

They were everywhere. Everywhere! How were we going to stop them? How could we even try? If they could take my own brother from me, if they could take Tom, then how was I going to be able to stop them? It was insane. Marco was right.

I think if I had been fully human right then, despair would have just overpowered me. But dogs don't know about human despair. It was Homer's simple, happy, hopeful mind that saved me. For a while I just sort of let go and drifted into dog consciousness. I didn't want to think. I didn't want to be a human being. For a while I just wandered around the dunes and smelled things.

But I knew I had a job to do. After a while I let go of the simple happiness of the dog and forced myself back into painful reality.

I waited and listened some more to the meeting. But I was still so upset I didn't really track on a lot of what was being said. I just kept hearing it over and over in my head — "Make him ours . . . or kill him."

The one other thing that did stick in my mind was Tom discussing with some other guy — some other *Controller* — the schedule for going to the Yeerk pool. He'd just been and was feeling good, he said. He'd be heading back on Monday night.

That was the slug in his head talking. The Yeerk that controlled Tom needed to return to the Yeerk pool.

Then I heard another voice. Cassie!

I slunk quickly around the back of a dune to get closer. But I could hear clearly. Cassie's voice, and another voice it took me a minute to recognize.

It was the policeman. The same policeman.

"Hey, what are you doing back here?" the policeman demanded.

"I was just looking for shells," Cassie said.

"This is just for full members," the policeman said gruffly. "Private business. You understand?"

"Yes, sir," Cassie said in her most humble voice.

I got to where I could see them, although I have to tell you, dog sight is not exactly great. Everything is like an old TV with bad color and all blurry.

The policeman was staring hard at Cassie. Cassie was trying to be brave, but I could smell the fact that she was afraid.

"Okay, take off," the policeman said at last. "But I have my eye on you. Get back with the others."

Cassie turned and headed away as fast as she could walk. I caught up with her. I guess seeing a dog come bounding out of nowhere startled her, because she jumped.

"Oh, it's you," she said.

<Yeah. That was close. What were you doing there?>

She shrugged. "Just wanted to make sure you were okay."

<I was safer than you were,> I pointed out.

We got back to the spot where Rachel, Marco, and Tobias were waiting. I didn't even want to morph back into my human body. I knew that I could just let myself go again, and in a few minutes my dog brain would forget why my human brain was sad. If someone would just throw a stick out into the surf I could go after it. The water would make me happy. The chasing would make me happy.

Now I knew why Tobias was so reluctant to leave his hawk's body. Being an animal could be a nice way to escape from all your troubles.

I began to morph back into my own body. Cassie and Rachel turned and looked out toward the water.

When I was completely myself again, I said, "Marco, you were right. Tom is a Controller."

Marco did not look pleased about being right.

I told them what Tom had said to Chapman about bringing me to the meeting to either use me or kill me.

"Wait a minute. Chapman is one of them, too?" Rachel asked. "Our Chapman? Mr. Chapman, the assistant principal?"

"I think he's some kind of a leader," I said. "It was him the other night at the construction site. He was the one who told the Hork-Bajir just to keep the head."

"That is *so* Chapman," Marco said.

"I suggest we get the heck out of here," Tobias said.

"No, it's okay," I said. "Chapman told Tom there was not to be any killing at a Sharing meeting. They don't want any suspicious activities. He also said they couldn't just go around killing every kid who *might* have been at the construction site. They needed to be sure."

"That's decent of them," Rachel said dryly.

"Not really. Chapman just said that for a while longer they still have to avoid attracting too much attention. A bunch of kids start turning up dead and people will definitely notice. He said they should just wait—kids can't keep quiet for long about seeing aliens. When the kids talk, the Controllers will find them and get rid of them."

"Except that we aren't going to talk about what we saw," Rachel said.

"You got that right," Marco agreed. "We aren't saying anything. We are forgetting everything we saw. We are getting on with our normal lives."

"And leave Tom the way he is?" I demanded. "No way. Never. He's my brother. I'm going to save him."

"Just how do you figure you'll do that?" Marco asked sarcastically. "Let's see, it's you versus Chapman, the cops, a bunch of Hork-Bajir and Taxxons, and, worst of all, that creep, Visser Three. All you can do to fight them is turn into a dog and bite their ankles. It's like being stuck in the most impossible video game ever invented."

I grinned. Or at least I showed my teeth. "Yeah, it is, kind of. But I'm pretty good at video games."

"And he won't be alone," Rachel said. "I'm in this, too."

"And me," Tobias said.

"Me, too," Cassie agreed.

"Swell," Marco said. "So suddenly you're the Fantastic Four. This isn't a comic book. This is real."

We heard the sound of people coming through the dunes. The meeting of the full members had broken up.

"Everyone, quiet," I said. "We'll let this ride . . . for now." I said that to calm Marco down. I had no intention of letting it ride.

I pulled Cassie aside. "Listen, Cassie, I need an animal morph that will let me watch Chapman without him seeing me. What do you have at the farm?"

Cassie got quiet for a moment. "Let me think. We have a lot of injured birds, of course. We have the wolf with the broken leg. We have the wildcat with one eye."

I waited while she went down a list of all the animals in the Wildlife Rehabilitation Clinic.

Suddenly Cassie snapped her fingers. "I wonder. . . . How small an animal do you think we can morph?"

I shrugged. I had no idea.

"I may have something in mind," she said. "It's not really in the clinic as a patient. It just sort of lives there. It's small. It can crawl up walls. It's fast, if you need to get away. And I guess it can hear and see okay."

Which is how I ended up in Cassie's barn later that night, crawling beneath cages full of sick buzzards and between a pair of jumpy deer, looking for lizards.

CHAPTER 16

I did it Monday morning in my locker at school. I turned into a lizard.

A green anole, to be exact. It's a member of the iguana family. Like you care.

I waited till the bell rang for first period, which was English class. When everyone else was out of the hallway, I just climbed into my locker. I tried to act cool about it, just in case anyone was watching.

The locker was about two inches shorter than me, so I had to crouch. And it was so tight I couldn't move. The only light was from the three small ventilation slits. I could hear my heart pounding in the cramped, dark space. I was afraid.

It was one thing to turn into a dog. I mean, it's weird, it's strange, but it's also kind of cool. Dogs are cool animals. But lizards?

"I should have practiced," I muttered under my breath. "I really should have practiced like Cassie said."

I started to focus for the morphing. I remembered the way we had caught the lizard the night before last. We'd spotted it with a flashlight, and Cassie had put a bucket over it so it couldn't get away.

It had been fairly creepy, just touching it to acquire its DNA pattern. Now I was going to *become* it.

The first thing I noticed was that I suddenly had more room inside the locker. I didn't have to crouch down. And my shoulders weren't scrunched up anymore.

I touched my face with one hand. My skin was looser than it should have been. And pebbly to the touch.

I ran my hand over my head. My hair was almost all gone.

Things began to happen very fast. The locker grew and grew around me. It was big as a barn. Big as a stadium!

It was like falling. Like falling off a skyscraper and taking forever to hit the ground.

I was standing on something sticky, as large as a boulder. How had a boulder gotten into my locker? But then I realized—it was a wad of gum! An old, chewed wad of gum stuck to the bottom of my locker.

Gigantic drapes as big as the sails of a ship were falling all around me. They were my clothes. In the dim light I could see two monstrous, misshapen things on either side of me. I could just make out the Nike swoosh, and realized they were my shoes. They were the size of houses.

And then the lizard brain kicked in.

Fear! Trapped! Run! Run! Rruunrunrun!

I shot left. A wall! I scampered up, feeling my feet stick to it. *Trapped!* I jumped back. Another hard surface. *Trapped! Runrunrunrun!*

I fought to get control, but the lizard brain was panicked. It didn't know where it was. It wanted out. *OUT!*

Go toward the light! I ordered my new body. The ventilation slits. That was the way out.

But the body was afraid of the light. It was terrified.

I was still bouncing off the walls. I could not overcome the panic instincts of the lizard body.

Go to the light! I screamed inside my head. And suddenly I was there. I poked my head out, and my body slithered after me. My tongue flicked out and I got a weird kind of input from it. Like smell, only not quite. It kept flicking. I could see it shoot out of my mouth and lick the air.

In the bright light I realized how bad the lizard eyes were. I couldn't make sense of what I was seeing. Everything was shattered and twisted around. Down was up and up was down. Colors weren't even close to right.

I tried to think. Come on, Jake. You have eyes on the side of your head now. They don't focus together. They see different things. Deal with it.

I tried to make sense of the pictures, using this knowledge, but they were still a mess. It seemed to take me forever to figure it out. One eye was looking down the hall to the left. The other was looking down the hall to the right. I was upside down, gripping the side of the locker, which was like a long, gray field that wouldn't end.

And all the time the green anole brain was fighting me. Now that it was out of the dark locker, it desperately wanted to go back in.

Chapman's office, I reminded myself. But where was it?

Left. That way.

Suddenly I was off and running. Straight down the wall. Zoom! Then on level floor. Zoom! Around a scrap of paper twice as big as I was. The ground flew past. It was like being strapped onto a crazy, out-of-control missile.

Then my lizard brain sensed the spider. It was a strange thing, like I wasn't sure if I saw the spider, or heard it, or smelled it, or tasted it on my flicking lizard tongue, or just suddenly *knew* it was there.

I took off after it, racing at a million miles an hour before I could even think about stopping. My legs were a blur, they moved so fast.

It probably wasn't a huge spider. Not if you were a great big human being. But to my lizard eyes it looked as big as a small child. It was huge. I could see the multiple black eyes. I could see the individual joints in its eight legs. I could see the clicking, awful mandibles.

The spider ran. I ran after it. I was faster.

Noooooooooooo! I screamed inside my head. But too late. My head jerked forward, fast as a striking snake. My jaws snapped. And suddenly the spider was in my mouth.

I could feel it fighting. I could *feel* the spider's legs squirming and fighting to get out of my mouth.

I tried to spit it out, but I couldn't. The lizard's hunger for that spider was too great.

I swallowed the spider. It was like swallowing a whole canned ham. A canned ham that was fighting all the way down.

No, no, no! my brain cried in horror and disgust. But at the same time, the lizard brain was pleased. I could feel it become slightly calmer.

That does it! I told myself. I am *out* of this morph!

I wanted out of that horrible little body. I didn't care who saw me, I was going to morph back to human shape. Marco was right. It was insane to get involved in this. Insane!

I heard the ground shake. It was a noise like a giant stomping across the land.

It *was* a giant.

There was a huge shadow in the sky. It was like someone was trying to crush me by dropping an entire building on my head.

The shoe came down!

I scampered left.

Another shoe.

My tail! The shoe was on my tail! I was trapped!

CHAPTER 17

In panic, I tried to run. But my tail was caught.

Suddenly I was free! How had that . . .

I realized what had happened. My tail had snapped off. Looking back, I saw it, still trapped by the giant shoe. It squirmed as if it were still alive. It wiggled like a worm on a hook.

The shoe lifted and flew through the air again.

I shot up the side of the wall and froze in place.

The giant had not seen me. It had not tried to stomp me. It had been an accident. And now my tail . . . no, the lizard's tail . . .

The giant walked on, shaking the ground as it went.

I focused one lizard eye on the figure. It was like trying to make sense out of one of those carnival fun mirrors. But even so, I was pretty sure it was Chapman.

I watched him head down the hall. And with all my power, I ordered my lizard body to follow him.

I tried not to think about the spider in my stomach, or the fact that it was still not completely dead. I tried not to think about the fact that part of my body was back on the floor, jerking like it was still alive. I just raced along after Chapman.

Because Chapman might reveal something that would help Tom.

I planned to follow Chapman to his office. I'd hide under his desk and listen to him make phone calls. I figured sooner or later he might let something slip about the location of the Yeerk pool.

Cassie and I had talked about it. She'd said it could take days of hiding in Chapman's office before we learned anything. Besides, we could only stay in a morph for two hours. And meanwhile, I would be skipping class. Sooner or later, I'd get in trouble over that.

And the really funny thing is, when they catch you skipping class, you get sent to the assistant principal.

Mr. Chapman.

I could just imagine *that* scene. . . . Sorry I skipped class, Mr. Chapman, but I've been in this lizard body, watching you because I know you're a Controller and part of a giant alien conspiracy to take over the earth.

I would have laughed, only lizards can't laugh. So I just followed Chapman as he marched down the hall.

Suddenly he stopped. Were we at his office?

I looked around as well as I could. It didn't look like the office. The spider gave a kick in my stomach.

He opened a door. It swung right over me with a big rush of air. It went just above my head as I hugged the floor.

I concentrated on making sense of the sights. Wait a minute! This was the janitor's closet, a mess of mops and buckets and cleaning solutions. What was Chapman doing . . . ?

He went inside. I followed, careful to stay away from the high leather walls that were his shoes.

I heard a loud click. He had locked the door behind him.

It was a long way up from the floor, but I could more or less see him doing things to the sink faucet.

I thought he grabbed one of the hooks they used to hang up the dirty mop heads. I was pretty sure he twisted it because I could hear a squeaking sound.

And to my total and complete amazement, the wall opened.

There was a doorway where the wall had been. Strange smells and stranger sounds wafted up from inside the doorway.

Chapman stepped through. There were stairs just inside, heading down into a purple-lit pit. From far away, as if it came from a hundred miles down, I heard a faint sound.

It was a scream. A scream of fear and despair. A human voice, crying out in the darkness of that horrible place.

"Noooo!" the voice moaned. "Noooo!"

I knew what the scream meant. I knew what was happening. Somewhere down there, a human being was feeling the Yeerk slug slither inside its brain. Somewhere down there, a human being was being turned into a mindless slave of the Yeerks.

Chapman headed down the stairs.

The door closed behind him.

I had found the Yeerk pool.

It was right under my school.

CHAPTER 18

Screams," I said. "Human screams. They sounded far off, but that's what they were."

My friends looked at me. All but Marco, who looked away. It was that same afternoon, right after school. We'd gone to the mall. We figured it was the best way not to look suspicious. No one thinks there's anything weird about kids hanging together at the mall.

We were at a table in the food court, sharing some nachos. Ever since eating the spider, I'd had a desire to consume lots of junk food to help me forget.

"You were a lizard at the time," Marco pointed out. "Who knows what you heard?"

"I know," I said.

"I can't stand the thought of what's happening to people down there," Cassie said. She shuddered. "It's sickening."

"We have to do something," Rachel said.

"Yeah, let's rush right down there," Marco said. "Then it can be *us* screaming."

I realized I had lost my appetite for nachos.

"Marco, you can't just ignore what's going on," Rachel said.

"Sure I can," he said. "All I have to do is remind myself that hey, guess what? I don't want to die."

"That's it, then?" Rachel demanded, outraged. "Just whatever is best for Marco?"

"I don't think Marco is being selfish," Cassie said. "Just the opposite. He's thinking about his father. About what would happen to his dad if Marco . . ."

"He's not the only one who's got people to worry about," Rachel said. "I have a family. We all do."

"Not me," Tobias said softly. He smiled his sad, crooked smile. "It's true. No one gives a rat's rear about me."

"I do," Rachel said.

I was surprised to hear her say that. Rachel isn't exactly sentimental.

"Look," I said. "I'm not asking anyone else to go with me. But I don't have a choice. I heard that scream today. And I know Tom is going down there tonight. He's my brother. I have to try and save him." I held out my hands, helpless. "I have to do it. For Tom."

"I'll go with you," Tobias said. "For the Andalite."

"There's no one else who can do anything to stop the Yeerks," Rachel said. "I'm scared to death, just thinking about it. But I'm there."

Marco looked sick. He gave me a dirty look. He shook his head. "This is bad," he said. "This is so bad. If it wasn't for Tom I'd walk away."

"Look, Marco, you don't have to—" I started to say.

"Oh, shut up!" he snapped. "You're my best friend, you jerk. Like I'm going to let you go face all this alone? I'm in. I'm in, to rescue Tom. That's it. Then I'm done."

Only Cassie had remained silent. She was looking dreamily off over the heads of the mall crowd. "You know, back in the old days—I mean, the real, *real* old days—the Africans, the early Europeans, the Native Americans . . . they all believed animals had spirits. And they would call on those spirits to protect them from evil. They would ask the spirit of the fox for his cunning. They'd ask the spirit of the eagle for his sight. They would ask the lion for his strength.

"I guess what we're doing is sort of basic. Even though it was Andalite technology that made it possible. We're still just scared little humans, trying to borrow the mind of the fox, and the eyes of the eagle . . . or the hawk," she added, smiling at Tobias. "And the strength of the lion. Just like thousands of years ago, we're calling on the animals to help protect us from evil."

"Will their strength be enough?" I wondered.

"I don't know," Cassie admitted solemnly. "It's like all the basic forces of planet Earth are being brought into the battle."

Marco rolled his eyes. "Nice story, Cassie. But we're five normal kids. Up against the Yeerks. If it was a football game, who would you bet on? We're toast."

"Don't be so sure," Cassie said. "We're fighting for Mother Earth. She has some tricks up her sleeves."

"Good grief," Marco said. "Let's all buy Birkenstocks and go hug some trees."

We all laughed, including Cassie.

"Cassie is right about one thing," Rachel said seriously. "The only thing we have going for us is this animal morphing thing. And so far the only morphs we've acquired are a cat, a bird, a dog, a horse, and a lizard. I think we need a little more firepower. We should head for The Gardens. We need to acquire more DNA—from some animals that are not going to be easy to acquire."

I nodded. "Yeah. I don't think the hawk, horse, and lizard team is going to impress the Yeerks. Rachel's right. I think we have to head to The Gardens. We need to get some help from Mother Earth's toughest children." I looked to Cassie. "Can you get us in?"

"I can get in free," she said. "You guys will have to pay, but I can use my mom's employee discount, so it'll be cheaper."

"Oh, I'm sure we could talk them into letting us in for nothing," Marco said. "Just tell them we're Animorphs."

"Tell them we're what?" Rachel asked.

"Idiot teenagers with a death wish," Marco said.

"Animorphs." I tried the word out. It sounded okay.

CHAPTER 19

We left straight from the mall, hopping a bus out to The Gardens, which is clear across the city. On the way, I tried to catch up on my homework. I had missed a lot of classes that day, so I borrowed class notes from my friends. Rachel kept perfect notes. Tobias had terrible notes with all kinds of little drawings in the margins. It took a while before I could figure out what they were. They were buildings and people and cars, the way they looked from high up in the sky.

"I don't really need to go in," Tobias said as we pooled our limited cash to buy tickets. "I'm happy with just my hawk morph. I don't want to be anything else."

"I think that's a mistake," Rachel said. "Our one real weapon is the power to morph. We should acquire as many useful morphs as we can."

"What kind of animal morphs are going to be able to deal with Visser Three when he turns into that big monster that ate the Andalite?" I asked. There was nothing in this zoo or any other that was going to kick that big monster's butt.

Marco winked. "Fleas? No one can kill fleas. We'll itch him to death."

I had to smile. "So now you're suddenly Mr. Hopeful?"

"No, I'm just so scared I'm getting weird," he said. "I haven't done this morphing stuff. You guys all have. I'm not even a full-fledged Animorph yet. I'm still normal."

"I still *feel* normal," Cassie said. She looked troubled.

"Cassie, you can turn into a horse," Marco said. "Very few normal kids can do that. It's different for Jake, turning into a lizard. He's always been a reptile."

I took a good-natured swing at Marco, but he dodged it. It was cool having Marco with us—even if he was giddy.

It took about a half an hour to reach the main gate of The Gardens. I climbed down off the bus feeling nervous—not at all like I usually felt going there. I mean, The Gardens is just about my favorite place to go, normally. But normally I'm not going there to get personal with dangerous animals.

The main part of The Gardens is rides. They have all the usual stuff, like roller coasters, which are my personal favorite, and Ferris wheels and water slides.

But they also have an animal part, which is like a zoo, only cooler. They do dolphin shows, and there's this whole section where you can get close to some of the safer animals. And this monkey habitat they have is like a whole monkey city, practically. Anyway, if I were an animal, and I had to be in a zoo, I'd want to be there.

Cassie led us to the main building, which holds all kinds of exhibits. It has everything but the really big animals that need lots of space. Those animals are farther out, mostly, in big grassy habitats that look like parks. Parks with walls and moats and fences around them.

The main building is supposed to be like a rain forest, I guess. It's where they keep animals that need to be warm all the time. There's a pathway that winds around with tall tropical trees overhead, with bushes here and there between the exhibits.

Some of the exhibits are tiny, and some are really big, like the area they have for otters. It has a waterfall and a water slide for the otters to play in.

We were near the otter habitat when Cassie stopped. "Okay, now everyone stay together, and try not to be too suspicious-looking," she said. "I'm taking you inside."

"Inside where?" Marco asked.

"Well, the way it works is, there are walkways behind all these exhibits. That's how they feed the animals and give them meds or whatever. Meds are medicines. Sorry." She pointed to an inconspicuous doorway. "Anyway, we can go in through there."

It was an odd change from outside to inside. One minute, we were in this fake rain forest. The next minute, we were in what looked like a hallway at school. Only the smell was worse — kind of damp and moldy and musty. More like the boys' locker room.

"Okay, look, if any staff people stop us, the story is we're here to see my mom," Cassie said. "Of course, it's so late in the afternoon she won't be here. I hope. Because if she finds out I've been dragging four of my friends around back here . . . Well, I can't be saving the world from alien invaders if I'm grounded. Hopefully, there won't be many staff people here at all."

We shuffled along the hallway, feeling like we definitely did not belong. Which we didn't. On either side of the main hall, there were paths that led to the different exhibits. Unfortunately, the doorways to the exhibits just had numbers on them. I knew we'd have to rely on Cassie's knowledge to find our way around. Behind some of those doors were animals you didn't want to just walk in on.

"How do you guys feel about gorillas?" Cassie said. She had stopped by one of the numbered doors. "This is Big Jim's cage. He just came over from another zoo, so he's in his own private environment for now. He's very gentle."

Slowly it dawned on me what Cassie was saying. "Oh. You mean, does one of us want to acquire his DNA?"

"That is why we're here, Jake," Rachel pointed out. She batted her eyes at Marco. "How about you, Marco? Haven't you always wanted to be a big, hairy guy?"

Marco didn't look like he was crazy about the idea. But I knew how to handle him.

"Maybe Marco should try something easier for his first morph," I said. "You know, like a cuddly little koala or something."

That did it.

"Koala?" Marco said, giving me a dirty look. "Open that door, Cassie." He hesitated. "You said gentle, right?"

"Gorillas are extremely gentle," Cassie said. Then, in a quieter voice, she added, "Unless you make them mad."

Cassie opened her backpack. She took out an apple and handed it to Marco. "Here. You just open the door. The way it's set up, none of the visitors will be able to see you unless you walk clear out into the cage. Besides, there's an extra security gate, so he can't just jump out and you can't just walk in. So we just open the door, and hope Big Jim feels like eating."

Behind the door was a second door of steel bars, with a little cutaway section for the handlers to shove the food through. The entire door opening was concealed behind a fake rock ledge so it wasn't visible to the people looking into the cage. But Big Jim noticed us right away. He climbed heavily down from his perch on a rock ledge and took a good look at us through the bars.

Big Jim was definitely *big*. He had fingers the size of my wrist. But Jim didn't seem to mind us being there. Mostly he seemed interested in Marco's apple. He looked Marco over, snorted like he wasn't impressed, and then held out his hand.

"Hand him the apple," Cassie directed. "He wants the apple."

"I loved your work in *King Kong versus Godzilla*," Marco told the ape. He stuck his hand through the bars and held out the apple. With surprising daintiness, the gorilla lifted the apple and began inspecting it closely.

"Hold his hand," I said.

"Yeah, right," Marco laughed.

"When you acquire DNA, the animal goes into a kind of trance," I said. "Go ahead, grab his hand and concentrate."

Marco tentatively touched the gorilla's wrist. "Nice monkey." The gorilla ignored him. Big Jim was much more interested in the apple than in any of us.

"Concentrate," Rachel urged.

Marco closed his eyes. The ape closed his eyes.

"This is so cool," Tobias commented. "You realize that gorilla could pull Marco apart like he was a paper doll. Look at those arms!"

Marco opened one eye. "Tobias? Being terrified gets in the way of concentrating. So how about if you shut up about his arms?"

Suddenly I heard a whirring sound. I looked down the hall, then back. It was one of those electric carts, like a golf cart. It was coming toward us.

"Just act natural," Cassie hissed. Marco slipped out and she slammed the door on Big Jim. "As long as it isn't a security guy, we're probably okay."

The cart came up to us. Its driver was a man wearing a stained tan lab coat over his jeans. In the back of the cart were two large white plastic buckets full of something brown and horrible-smelling. "Hey, you're Cassie, right? The doc's kid? How's it going?"

"Fine," Cassie said. She waved casually, and the man drove right on past.

"That was easy," Rachel said. "He didn't even seem to care that we're back here."

"Well, where next?" Cassie wondered. We were at a four-way corner. There were blank, white-painted hallways in all directions. An electric golf cart was parked there, too.

"What are we near?" I asked.

Cassie thought for a moment. "Okay, that walkway leads to the outer exhibits. That one leads to the offices and storage facilities. These two go around the main building exhibits. We're close to . . . let me see . . . um, bats and snakes that way. The jaguar and the dolphin tank that way."

Rachel started down the hallway to our right. "Dolphins. I love dolphins."

"Wait," Cassie said, trotting after her. "What are we going to do with dolphin morphs?"

"I think we should go out to the big exhibits," Marco said. "Let's get serious about this. We need firepower. Come on."

"Let's stick together," I said as Marco started down the hall. I reached out to grab him before he got too far away.

And that's when the voice yelled, "Hey! Hey, you! What are you kids doing back here?"

I saw a guy in a brown uniform.

"Security!" Cassie yelped. "Oh, man, they'll take us all into the office. They'll call my mom. I do *not* want to explain this to her."

"Split up!" I said, trying to sound like a leader. "Just like at the construction site: One guy can't get us all!"

"This guy looks like my grandfather," Rachel said. "Not like that Hork-Bajir that was after us."

"You kids hold on!"

"Oh, man. Oh, man," Cassie said. With that, she took off down one hallway. Rachel and Tobias went after her.

Marco was already twenty yards down the other hall, the one that led out to the large exhibits. I ran to catch up.

The guard reached the corner. I saw him glance toward Tobias and the girls. Then he looked at me and Marco. I guess Marco and I looked more suspicious, because he chose us.

"Stop! You kids better stop!"

"Let's grab the golf cart!" Marco said.

"Steal a golf cart?"

"If we don't take it, that guard will."

"Good point."

We jumped in the cart. Marco slid behind the wheel. He turned the key to "on." He looked at me. "Just like driving bumper cars, right?"

"Only you try *not* to hit anything."

He put his foot down on the pedal. The electric motor made a whirring sound, and we took off. Straight toward the wall.

Bam!

"Hey, try steering," I yelled.

We backed up and took off again. We picked up speed. Enough to pull away from the guard, but when I looked back, he was still jogging after us.

"He's going to have a heart attack," I said.

"Which way?"

"What?"

"Which *way*?"

I turned around to face forward. We had reached a T-corner. "Right!" I yelled.

Naturally, Marco turned left. I nearly fell out.

Almost immediately, we reached another corner. This time Marco did choose right. And I *did* fall out of the cart.

I hit the linoleum and rolled. Then I was up and racing to catch the cart.

"What are you doing?" Marco demanded when he saw me. "Quit playing around."

I just gave him a dirty look and climbed back in.

"I think we lost the guard," Marco said.

"I'm fine, thanks for asking," I said. "Just a few bruises. Maybe a cracked skull. Nothing serious."

"Where do you think we are?"

"I think we are in the longest tunnel I've ever seen," I said. It was more and more like a tunnel now. The floor was still linoleum and the walls were still whitewashed, but the lights were getting more spread out, so you definitely had the feeling you were underground.

"I wonder if they caught the others," Marco said. "Now do you see why it's crazy to think we can beat the Yeerks? I mean, come on: We can barely beat zoo security."

"We haven't beat anyone yet," I said grimly. "Look!"

Way up ahead, there were two guys in brown uniforms.

"Maybe they don't know who we are," Marco suggested. "They might think we're regular employees."

"Maybe. But not if they get a good look at us." I pointed. "There's a turnoff. Take it."

We turned. At the same time, the guards started

yelling. The side corridor grew narrow. Too narrow for the golf cart.

"Ditch it!" I jumped out. Marco jumped after me. We could hear the guards' footsteps as they ran down the main tunnel. These guys were in better shape than the old man. These guys could run.

The corridor ended abruptly. There were two doors, one a little to the left, one a little farther to the right. They were labeled P-201 and P-203. No help at all.

"Pick a door," Marco said.

I took a deep breath. "Door number one." I opened P-201. A blast of fresh air hit me. Sunlight blinded me. I blinked, trying to get my eyes to adjust.

The rhinoceros blinked, too. "Ahhhh!" I yelled.

"Ahhhh!" Marco yelled.

We jumped back and slammed the door.

"Wrong door!" Marco said.

"Definitely wrong!" I agreed.

"Hey, you kids! Stop right there!"

The guards were just at the end of the corridor.

"Gotta try door number two!" I said.

"Do it!"

We opened the door and ran through.

There were trees all around us. Trees and grass. We were in the shade. Sunlight filtered down through the leaves. Just ahead the bushes gave way to open grass.

"Where are we?" Marco asked.

"Like I know?"

We worked our way through some bushes, keeping a careful eye out in all directions. We didn't see any animals. Just some birds up in the trees.

"Hey, there are people!" Marco said. He dropped down behind a bush and pointed.

There were people lined up behind a railing. They were high up. Or else we were low down. I parted the bushes to get a better look. The people were leaning against a railing at the top of a high concrete wall. They couldn't see us because of the bushes. But they were definitely all staring at *something*.

"We're definitely in one of the habitats," I said. "Those are people looking at . . . at whatever is in here with us. I'm just hoping it isn't that rhino. That thing was *way* too big."

"How do we get out of here?"

"I don't know, let's just get away from the door. Those guards will be coming after us any second." But, you know, in the back of my mind I was thinking, Hmm, why *haven't* those guards come after us yet?

Marco and I crawled through the bushes and around the bases of the big trees. We reached a corner of the wall, hidden from all the people above.

"That is an awfully high wall," Marco observed. "That's got to be thirty feet high. This is not good.

That wall is high for a reason. There's something in here that they don't want to escape."

I scanned the wall. There was a steel ladder set into the concrete about fifty yards away. "I guess that's the only way out."

"Let me ask you something," Marco said. "Why haven't the guards come after us? I mean, if this was, like, the deer and antelope exhibit, they'd come right in, wouldn't they?"

"We have to think, not panic," I said. "I am trying *not* to think about why the guards didn't come in here." I moved back into the shadows of the bushes. "Besides, maybe there's nothing in here at all."

I squatted down on my haunches.

My butt touched something warm.

I had a terrible feeling right at that moment. I looked up and saw Marco. Normally, Marco has kind of a dark, tanned face. But his face was white. And his eyes were very large.

"Marco," I said, very slowly and very quietly, "is there something behind me?"

He nodded.

"What is it, Marco?"

"Um . . . Jake? It's a tiger."

CHAPTER 20

A male Siberian tiger, to be exact. Ten feet long. Seven hundred pounds of deadly speed and unbelievable power.

You know those old Tarzan movies you see on TV sometimes, where Tarzan is wrestling a tiger? And actually winning? Let me tell you something. You want to know what your chances are of wrestling a tiger and coming out alive? They're about the same as your chances of jumping off the Empire State Building and surviving.

"I have an idea," Marco said shakily. "Let's leave."

"Don't run," I said. "It might just get his attention."

"I think he's noticed us," Marco said. "I think he knows we're here, Jake. I think he's looking right at us! Look at his teeth!"

"Don't freak! I have an idea. The morphing. If I acquire him, it'll put him in a trance."

"Acquire? Acquire what? You can't acquire anything about *him*. He's the acquir*er*, and you're the acquir*ee*. He's going to acquire your butt for dinner! He's going to acquire you and spit out the bones."

I swallowed hard. I tried to touch the tiger, but my hand was shaking too much. I took a couple of deep breaths. I heard somewhere that's supposed to calm you down. I guess it works. Unless you're practically sitting on a tiger. Then absolutely *nothing* calms you down.

"Nice tiger," I whispered.

He just watched me. He had this lazy "who cares?" look. This look of total, complete, absolute confidence. Almost like he thought I was funny. Like maybe he enjoyed watching me shiver and shake.

"Please don't kill me," I said.

"Don't kill me, either," Marco added.

I reached my shaking hand toward the tiger. His eyes followed my hand. I touched his flank. It rose and fell with his breathing.

142

"Concentrate," Marco whispered.

I was already concentrating real hard on the tiger. I was concentrating on his teeth. I was concentrating on the rippling muscles under his pale orange and black pelt. I was totally concentrating on the fact that he could swing that big, massive paw of his and send my head flying across the grass like a soccer ball.

Then the tiger's breathing slowed. His eyes fluttered a little and slowly closed.

"How long does the trance last?" Marco whispered.

"Well, about ten seconds after you break contact. That's what it was with Homer."

"Ten seconds? Ten seconds?"

"Yeah. So be ready to run."

"I've *been* ready to run!"

I started to pull away, but then I hesitated. It was a strange moment, because right then I realized what I was doing. It hit me. This tiger was becoming part of me. All that power and confidence was becoming part of *me*.

"He's beautiful, isn't he?" I said.

I expected Marco to say something sarcastic. But he said, "Yes. He's magnificent." Then he added, "But let's get out of here before he shows us why he's king of the jungle."

"That's lions," I said. "They're supposed to be king of the jungle. But let's not tell *him* that. You ready?"

He nodded.

"Now!" I yelled.

I jumped up and we tore for the ladder. In my head I was counting off the seconds: one–one thousand, two–one thousand, three–one thousand . . .

Something moved. Fast! An orange and black blur!

Right then I realized it. *Duh.* There was more than one tiger in the habitat.

I heard screams coming from the spectators above. I guess they could see us now that we were out of the bushes.

Marco leaped and grabbed the rungs of the ladder. He scrambled up. I was about one-tenth of a second behind him. The tiger leaped. His claws scraped the concrete just inches below me. And then he let out a roar that made the rungs of the ladder vibrate in my hands.

Ggggggrrrrraaaawwwrrrr!

What a noise! It echoed and reverberated and made my insides turn to liquid.

Marco practically flew up the ladder and over the side of the wall. I flew right after him.

It's amazing how fast you can climb a ladder when there's a tiger roaring for your blood.

"There they are!" someone yelled. "Get them. Stop!"

Guards! At least three of them.

"Should we morph?" Marco yelled to me.

"No! Just head for the crowds! There! Over by the dolphin tank."

It was a close call, but we made it to a big crowd just a dozen feet ahead of the guards.

From that point, all we had to do was hunch down and squirm between all the people till the guards lost sight of us. We worked our way to the front gate, always crouching so our heads wouldn't show above the crowds.

"What did you do, morph into a midget?" It was Rachel. She was right in front of me, looking amused. Tobias and Cassie were there, too.

"The guards were after us," I said. I had almost stopped shaking from my close encounter with the big cats. Almost.

"Oh, quit playing around, Jake," Rachel said. "Let's get out of here. I have to be home for dinner."

It turned out the other three had not been chased at all. They'd lost the guards easily, and had just gone on acquiring morphs while Marco and I were risking our lives in the tiger habitat.

The most annoying thing was that none of them even believed our story. Marco and I were a little resentful over that.

We climbed on board the bus and practically collapsed into the seats.

"We could have been killed," Marco said, pouting. "Really. I'm telling you. It was down to a few inches."

"Yeah, whatever," Rachel said. "Don't obsess over it. After all, we still have tonight to deal with. Whatever danger you think you had today, it will probably be nothing, next to what's going to happen tonight."

"Tonight." Cassie shook her head. "And I haven't even *thought* about studying for that math test tomorrow."

Rachel laughed. "We may not have to worry about tomorrow."

"Thank you, Little Miss Cheerful," Marco muttered under his breath.

CHAPTER 21

"Where have you been all afternoon and evening?" my mom asked me as we sat down for dinner. My family is very old-fashioned about dinner. We all have to sit at the table. No TV. My mom's a writer, so she hates TV unless it's one of her favorite programs.

"Where have I been?" I repeated the question. "Um . . . hanging out. You know. Hanging with Marco."

"I don't know why you bother to ask," my dad said. "His answer is always the same—hanging out."

"So what did you do at work today, Dad?" I asked him.

"Hung out," he said. He gave me a wink and we all laughed.

I glanced over at Tom. He was eating chicken cacciatore like the rest of us and laughing. He seemed so normal.

"You doing anything tonight, Tom?" I asked him.

"Why?"

I tried to look casual. "You know, I was thinking maybe we could shoot some hoops," I said. "Maybe you could teach me some new moves and I could take another shot at making the team."

"Sorry, man," he said. "I have things to do tonight."

"Yeah, like what?" I asked.

"Hanging out, no doubt," my mom said. "Eat the broccoli, Jake, it's good for you. It's full of trace minerals and vitamins you can't get anywhere else."

"Okay," I said to my mom. "You know how much I love trace minerals." I popped the smallest piece of broccoli I could find and tried to gag it down. I guess it wasn't any worse than eating a live spider.

"So, Tom, what was it you said you were doing?" I asked again.

He gave me a dirty look. "Do I have to check in with you now? I have things to do. Is that okay, little brother?"

"A girl," my dad commented. "I know these things. I'm a doctor."

No, Dad, not a girl, I wanted to say—a Yeerk pool. What's a Yeerk pool, Mom? Well, it's kind of a long story.

I decided to try one more time. I guess a part of me still refused to believe what Tom was. "Maybe you're just afraid to shoot hoops with me. Maybe I'd kick your butt."

"Yeah, that's it. Happy now?" Tom sneered.

His gaze met mine. Was there some sign in those eyes? Some evidence of the selfish, evil creature that was controlling him? No. I wish there had been.

But there is no way to know who is a Controller and who isn't. No way. It's what makes them so hard to stop. They can be anyone. Anywhere.

Even a person you think you know. A person you admire. Look up to. Love.

I broke my gaze away from Tom's and looked down at my food.

A few minutes later, Tom got up to go. I knew where he was going. After he left, I went to the upstairs phone, where my parents couldn't overhear me. I called Marco.

"He's on his way," I said.

I called Tobias and Rachel. I tried to call Cassie, but I got her mother instead.

"She's not in," her mom said. She sounded worried. "She wasn't home for dinner. She went out to feed some of the animals and didn't come back."

My stomach clenched.

"She's probably just out riding one of the horses," I said, trying to reassure myself as much as Cassie's mom. "You know Cassie."

"All the horses are in their stalls," she said.

I took a couple of deep breaths. Something was wrong. What had happened to Cassie?

"I'll look around for her," I said. "Don't worry. I'll bet she just saw some injured animal or something and went off to rescue it. You know Cassie," I said again.

"Yes, I'm sure she's fine."

Right. She was about as sure as I was. But what could I do? The plan was set to attack the Yeerk pool and rescue Tom. Maybe Cassie was already at the school, waiting.

Maybe.

I had a very bad feeling as I rode my bike to the school. I hid the bike across the street, the way we had planned. Then I hooked up with Marco and Rachel.

"Cassie's missing," I said. "And where's Tobias?"

Rachel pointed up at the sky. The sun was setting fast, but I could see Tobias circling high overhead.

"What is the matter with him?" I exploded. "He's got a two-hour time limit and we don't know how long this is going to take!"

"Maybe we should bail until we find out what happened with Cassie," Rachel said.

"Could be she's just scared," Marco said. "I am."

"Maybe," I agreed, although I doubted it. But they say you never know who's going to be brave or cowardly in a battle.

I just hoped I wasn't a coward. The truth was, my mouth was already dry and my heart was already pounding. And we hadn't even done anything yet.

Tobias swooped down and perched on Rachel's shoulder. It surprised me a little. Why would Tobias perch on Rachel's shoulder? And she didn't seem at all annoyed. She rubbed her head against him a little.

<Are we doing this, or not?> Tobias asked.

This was not starting off right at all. The bad feeling in my stomach was just getting worse. Cassie missing. Tobias already morphed.

Everyone was looking at me, waiting for me to decide.

"Yeah, we're doing it," I said.

The school was locked up for the night. But Marco had taken care of that little problem. He knew of a window in the science lab that didn't lock.

We crawled into the science lab through the window. It was dark, except for the dying light of the sun that glinted off the glass beakers and test tubes. Tobias drifted through and landed neatly on the teacher's desk.

"Let me take a look," I said. I opened the door as slowly as I could and peeked out through the crack. I could see down the nearly dark hallway to the janitor's closet. Instantly I pulled back in.

"There are people out there!" I said. "Three people heading into the closet."

"Controllers," Rachel said. "I guess it's dinnertime for Yeerks."

None of us thought that was very funny.

"How are we going to get in there?" Marco asked.

"Wait a minute," Rachel said. "Do all the Controllers know each other by sight? I mean, maybe we're Controllers, right?"

"So we just walk right on in like we belong there?" Marco asked. "Wonderful plan, Rachel. I have a better idea—let's just kill ourselves now and get it over with."

"Maybe Rachel's right," I said.

"Big maybe," Marco pointed out. "Big, *huge* maybe. How about Tom? He would know whether you were a Controller."

I cracked the door again and looked out. "I think Tom's already down there," I said. "Besides, the hallway's empty now. I guess they all . . ." I fell silent. "Wait, here comes someone."

I stared. It wasn't easy to see faces in the gloom. I could tell there were two people. One was wearing a uniform.

It was the Controller policeman. And he was rudely yanking someone along with him. I could see that it was a girl.

I didn't really want to see any more. "Tobias," I said. "I need you to use your hawk's eyes."

Tobias fluttered over and stood on my shoulder. He peeked his fierce head out into the hall and then drew back.

<Yes,> he said. <It's her.>

I felt like the floor had opened underneath me. Marco grabbed me because I looked like I was about to fall over.

"They have her!" I whispered. "The Controllers. They have Cassie!"

CHAPTER 22

"Who has Cassie . . . how?" Rachel stammered.

"That policeman. The Controller, the one who came out to Cassie's farm. The one who was at The Sharing meeting. He has her. He saw her at the meeting trying to get close to the full members."

Rachel let go a few choice words.

We hadn't even started and already everything was a disaster.

"Okay," I said grimly. "We go ahead, like Rachel said. We figure there are too many Controllers for all of them to know each other. I mean, they add new bodies all the time, right? So maybe we're new Controllers, right?"

"Oh, man," Marco moaned.

"You have a better idea?" I snapped.

"No," he said. "I think we go ahead. We take our chances. Let's rock and roll."

"Okay, then, everyone act cool." I looked at Tobias. "Too late for you to morph back now. But try not to let them see you."

Rachel, Marco, and I stepped out into the dark hallway. My legs were stiff. My knees were rickety. I was walking like Frankenstein's monster trying to look casual.

We headed for the janitor's closet. Fortunately, no one else was in the hallway.

We entered the tiny room and stepped inside. I tried to recall the sequence for opening the door. Faucet to the left, then twist the second hook around to the right.

The door swung open.

There was more noise than there had been the other day. Or maybe it was just that my human ears heard it better than my lizard ears had.

There was a deep sloshing, swooshing sound, almost like gentle surf breaking on the shore. But that was the nice sound. The other sounds were horrifying—despairing cries, terrified screams, shouts, shrieking triumphant laughter.

"You sure this is just the Yeerk pool?" Marco said in a nervous, shaky voice. "I see a guy with horns and a pitchfork and I am outta here."

I stepped into the opening. The stairs were steep and there was no rail, so you felt like you were about to pitch forward with every step.

We descended together. The door closed automatically behind us.

At first I guess I expected there to be maybe a couple dozen steps. But the steps never ended. We just kept walking, and there were always more steps. The walls were dirt, then quickly became rock as we went down, down, down. It felt like those stairs would never end.

"Some superior aliens," Marco whispered. "You'd think they could have put in an elevator."

We all giggled a little. Very little.

Suddenly, the rock walls widened out. We had emerged into a huge cavern.

And when I say huge, I mean huge. They could have played the Super Bowl in there *and* had room left over for a couple of malls. It was like a giant bowl turned upside down, all carved out of solid rock. At the very top of the bowl was the faint outline of a hole. I thought I could see stars through it.

All around the outer edges of the cavern I could see other stairways, like ours. They seemed to come from every direction, appearing out of the rock walls, and leading down to the floor of the cavern.

We clustered closer to the center of the stairway. It was a sheer drop off the side of the stairs.

"This is gigantic," Marco said. "This isn't just under the school. This is under half the town. Those stairways must lead up to a dozen secret entrances." He shook his head. "Jake, they have this entire area set up with secret passageways. Oh, man. This is worse . . . this is so much worse . . . so much bigger . . ."

I felt the same despair. We were fools. This wasn't some little group of alien bad guys we were dealing with. To build this underground city, these guys had power we couldn't even imagine.

That's almost what it was. A city.

There were buildings and sheds all around the rim of the cavern. And we could see yellow Caterpillar earthmovers and cranes at work on the far side of the cavern. They seemed weirdly normal in this incredible place.

And there were creatures everywhere. Taxxons, Hork-Bajir, and other things I couldn't even begin to guess at.

But mostly, there were humans. A lot of them.

At the very center of the cavern was a pool, like a small lake, maybe a hundred feet across, and perfectly round. Only the water wasn't exactly water. It moved more like melted lead, and was about the same color. The sloshing sound we could hear was the liquid of the pool being rippled and splashed by hundreds of fast-moving things below the surface.

I knew what they were. Yeerks. Yeerks in their natural, sluglike state. They were swimming and cavorting in the pool like kids on a hot day.

Near the edge of the pool were cages. In the cages were Hork-Bajir and human beings.

Some of the humans screamed for help. Some cried silently. Some just sat and waited, all hope lost. There were adults there. And kids. Women and men. More than a hundred, packed ten to a cage.

The captive Hork-Bajir were kept in separate, stronger cages. They paced and howled and slashed at the air with their bladed arms.

I almost lost hope. I felt like my heart had stopped. This was a place of unimaginable horror. And we were so few, and so weak.

Below us on the stairs I could see the Controller cop and Cassie. He was dragging her roughly whenever she stumbled. They had reached the bottom of the stairs.

"I'm going to morph," I said. "I'm going to get Cassie away from him."

Marco put his hand on my shoulder. "Not time yet, dude. Be cool."

<Cassie's okay, Jake,> Tobias said. <She isn't hurt. Just scared.>

"He'd better not hurt her," I said. "Keep an eye on them, Tobias."

There were two low steel piers built out over the pool. On one, Hork-Bajir-Controllers politely guarded a line of humans and Hork-Bajir and Taxxons.

This was the unloading station.

One by one the people knelt down, bent over, and dipped their heads toward the slimy surface of the pool. The Hork-Bajir helped them.

As we watched, a woman calmly bent over, her head just inches above the lead gray pool. A Hork-Bajir held her elbow gently, to help her keep her balance.

Then we saw the thing dribbling, sliding, squirming, crawling out of her ear.

A Yeerk.

"Oh, no . . ." Rachel moaned. She sounded like she might be sick. "Oh, no. No."

159

When the Yeerk was all the way out of the poor woman's head, it dropped into the pool and disappeared beneath the turbulent surface.

Instantly the woman cried out. "You filth, let me go! Let me go! I am a free woman! You can't keep doing this! I am not a slave! Let me go!"

Two Hork-Bajir grabbed her. They dragged the woman to the nearest cage and threw her in.

"Help!" the woman screamed. "Oh, please, someone help. Help us all!"

CHAPTER 23

"Help! Please, someone help us!"

We had been hearing cries like that all the way down those steps. But now we were close enough to give the cries a human face. It cut straight to my soul.

There was a second steel pier. That was the loading station. There the host bodies were dragged from their holding cages to have the Yeerks reenter their heads. It was a pretty basic process. They grabbed the hosts, whether human or Hork-Bajir, and forced their heads down into the pool.

The people sometimes fought and screamed, and sometimes just cried. But they always lost. When their heads were yanked back up out of the pool, we could see the slugs still slithering into their ears.

After a few minutes they would become calm again, as the Yeerks regained control. Then off they went, once more slaves of the Yeerks.

It was a horrible assembly line, from the unloading pier, to the holding cages, to the infestation pier. They moved the poor victims through at a pretty speedy rate.

But there was another area we could only now see. There, humans and Hork-Bajir waited on comfortable chairs, sipping drinks and actually watching TV. Taxxons squirmed around like gigantic, spiny maggots.

I heard the faint sound of a television set. I was sure I could hear laughter from the humans. They were watching the show and having a good laugh.

<Those are the voluntary hosts,> Tobias said. <Collaborators.>

"What are you talking about?" I demanded.

<You remember, what the Andalite told us. Many humans and Hork-Bajir are *voluntary* hosts,> Tobias replied. <The Yeerks persuade them to let them take over.>

"I can't believe that," Rachel said. "No person would ever *let* this happen to them. No one would ever give up control of himself."

"Some people are scum, Rachel," Marco said. "Sorry to burst your balloon."

<The Yeerks convince them that taking on a Yeerk will solve all their problems. I think that's what The Sharing is all about. People believe that by becoming something different, they can leave behind all their pain.>

"Like spending all their time as a hawk," Marco pointed out.

Tobias had nothing to say to that. He spread his wings and flew up and away.

"Tobias! Come back," I called to him.

"We have to get moving," Rachel said. "We've been standing here staring for too long." She looked at Marco. "Don't be a jerk to Tobias, okay? We need everyone."

Tobias came swooping back toward us. <Cassie,> he said. <She's on the pier. The infestation pier. They're going to turn her into a host.>

With my normal human eyes I couldn't see that well in the purple gloom. I could just make out the cop's uniform and the small shape beside him.

"Do you see Tom?" I asked Tobias.

In answer he flapped his powerful wings and gained altitude. I saw him high over the pool. Then he came back toward us in a power dive.

<I see him,> he said.

I hesitated before asking. I wasn't sure I wanted to know the answer. "Is he in the cages? Or is he . . . voluntary?"

<He's in a cage,> Tobias said. <He's yelling his brains out at the Hork-Bajir guards.>

"Yes!" I knew Tom would never have gone voluntarily. I knew they must have taken him kicking and punching.

<Cassie is getting near the end of the pier,> Tobias warned. <We only have a few minutes before they infest her!>

It was time. We were at the bottom of the steps.

We ran over to hide behind a storage shed of some kind. Marco pulled me around the corner, drawing me close so that I could hear him whisper. "Look, before we do this, there's one thing, Jake. You have to promise me."

I knew what he was going to say.

"If I have to die, okay. But don't let them take me. Don't let them put one of those things in my head."

"It'll be okay—"

"You!" a voice yelled. A human voice. "You two. Who are you?"

I spun around. A man. Just one man. But beside him, flanking him, was a big Hork-Bajir, looking suspicious. And on the other side, a Taxxon.

Somehow the man hadn't seen Rachel. She was

just around the corner of the building. But he had seen Marco and me talking. I guess it hadn't looked quite right to him.

"Us?" Marco asked. "Who are we? Hey, who are *you*?"

"Take them," the man ordered.

The Hork-Bajir advanced on us. The Taxxon slithered forward on its dozens of sharp, spiny legs, red jelly eyes quivering, mouth opening and closing in anticipation.

I knew I had to morph. But I was frozen with fear. Then I saw Rachel. She had gotten around behind the Controllers. And she was getting very, very large.

CHAPTER 24

Rachel was getting larger very fast. Huge leathery ears sprouted suddenly from the side of her head. Her nose stretched and stretched till it was longer than her body had been to start with. Her arms and legs were big as tree trunks. And from her mouth grew two enormous, curved teeth.

My cousin Rachel now stood almost thirteen feet high and weighed about fourteen thousand pounds.

The weird thing was, I was happy about all this.

<Ha HA!> I heard Rachel's triumphant laugh. <I did it.>

The Hork-Bajir and the Taxxon came closer.

Rachel began twitching her little ropy tail. Her

front legs pawed the dirt floor of the cavern. She raised her massive head and stuck out her three-foot-long tusks.

The Taxxon was the first to notice her with his all-around red-jelly eyes, but I guess he didn't know how to react.

Rachel charged. One minute she was standing there, and the next minute she was barreling forward like an out-of-control eighteen-wheeler.

The Hork-Bajir was fast. He spun around and slashed at her trunk with his elbow blade.

Too little. Too late.

Rachel was moving, and no little flesh wound was going to stop her.

<Puny little nothing!> Rachel cried, outraged. <You attack ME?!>

The Hork-Bajir went down, crushed under her monstrous feet. He bellowed, but Rachel's trumpeting was louder.

The Taxxon tried to run. It turns out Taxxons can move when they want to.

It also turns out elephants are faster than you think. They can be *very* fast.

Rachel's foot caught the Taxxon's back end. The needle legs collapsed, cracking like broken twigs. Yellow goo oozed from the popped flesh of the big worm.

She just kept rolling over him, leaving behind a big, extremely disgusting pile of goo. The foul smell of the squashed Taxxon nearly knocked me out.

The human was still just standing there. He said, "An elephant?" Like he couldn't even think about *it* being real.

Rachel wrapped her trunk around his middle.

<Yeah,> we heard Rachel say. <An elephant.>

The man screamed. I guess he figured out it was real.

Rachel threw him through the air. I never saw *where* he landed.

"Quick!" I yelled at Marco. "Morph!"

"Nice work, Rachel," Marco said. "Remind me not to ever make you mad."

I focused on the tiger. I knew his DNA pattern was in me. I thought of him, lying there in his habitat at The Gardens wishing he were back in the jungle, hunting and taking down his prey. I guessed maybe he wouldn't mind the use I was making of his DNA. This wasn't quite a jungle, but it would have to do.

<More Hork-Bajir coming!> Rachel said.

Rachel turned to face them, tusks ready.

I felt the morph begin. The hair grew from my face. The tail squirted out behind me. My arms bulged and rippled. They were massive! My shirt ripped. I fell forward onto my hands, now my front legs.

The power!

It was electric. It was like a slow-motion explosion. I could feel the power of the tiger growing inside me.

I watched claws, long, wickedly curved, tearing, ripping, shredding claws, grow from my puny human hands. I could feel the teeth sprouting in my mouth.

My eyes looked through the darkness like it was broad daylight.

But most of all, the power! The sheer, incredible power.

I was afraid of NOTHING!

Hork-Bajir were running at me, their arm blades slashing at the air.

I opened my mouth and I roared. The Hork-Bajir stopped dead in their tracks.

That's right, my little Hork-Bajir friends, the human part of my brain thought. *Time to meet the tiger.*

The muscles in my back legs coiled up. I bared my teeth and gave them another roar loud enough to make the ground quiver.

I leaped through the air, claws outstretched.

CHAPTER 25

I sailed through the air and struck the closest Hork-Bajir in the chest.

Down he went with me on top of him. He rolled over and tried to get up. He was fast. I was faster.

He struck at me with his razored arm. I ducked under the blow. My left paw swung, so fast even I couldn't see it. It left four oozing tracks across the Hork-Bajir's shoulder.

Another Hork-Bajir! Wrist blades, elbow blades, and talons whizzed. They were like a pair of lawn mowers on full throttle.

And still I was faster. I can't even remember what happened next. All I have is this image of the tiger—of me—with claws slashing and jaws snapping. I was a whirlwind of orange fur and black stripes.

The Hork-Bajir fell back. I roared. They turned and ran.

On one side I saw Rachel. She lifted a Hork-Bajir up on her tusks and tossed him back over her shoulder like he was a doll.

And then I saw Marco. Big Jim's massive body was ripping its way out of Marco's slight frame.

<Just call me King,> Marco said. <King Kong.>

The truth is, like Cassie said, gorillas are very gentle, peaceful, quiet creatures. The truth also is that they are strong. Real strong.

Basically, compared to a gorilla, a man is something made out of toothpicks.

Now, Hork-Bajir are pretty large creatures. They stand about seven feet high and are built for trouble. But Marco swung one big gorilla fist and hit the nearest Hork-Bajir in the stomach. The Hork-Bajir went down. Hard.

I roared. Rachel trumpeted. Marco lifted the Hork-Bajir up and tossed him aside like a rag doll.

The rest of the Hork-Bajir turned and ran.

<Now!> I shouted. <Before they get organized again!>

We charged. Rachel just plowed right through

some of the small sheds and buildings like Godzilla heading for Tokyo.

Marco came loping along, swinging his massive forearms, punching anything that got in his way. Whatever he punched stayed down.

And I ran right down the middle, looking for any Controller dumb enough to mess with me.

We reached the cages. The people and Hork-Bajir inside shrank back from us. They were almost as afraid of us as they were of the Controllers. Let's face it — a rescue party made up of an elephant, a gorilla, and a tiger is *not* what they'd been hoping for.

Marco began ripping at a lock on one of the cages. The lock gave way. The door flew open. Marco did something very human to reassure them. He made a little bow, then crooked his finger at them as if to say *come on out*.

Tom was the first out. He looked scared and mad and determined. I was going to send him a thought message, telling him who I was, but suddenly there was Rachel, screaming in my head.

<Jake!> Rachel said. <Look. Cassie!>

Cassie was nearly at the end of the infestation pier. The Hork-Bajir and Taxxon guards were still sticking to their duties. As I watched, another human was shoved headfirst into the Yeerk pool.

<Cassie is next!> I cried.

<Don't worry,> Marco said. <We'll take care of Tom. Go. Go before they do it to her!>

I hesitated for only a second, as a thousand thoughts went through my head.

Later I would think about that moment. Think maybe . . . maybe . . . if only . . .

I broke into a run. I had to get to her!

As I watched, the two Hork-Bajir on the pier grabbed Cassie by the arms.

"Nooooo!" she cried.

I tore at full speed. I leaped over Taxxons. I dodged around Hork-Bajir. I practically flew.

But I couldn't really fly. Not the way Tobias could.

I saw him high, high up in the cavern. Down he came.

Like a bullet.

The talons came forward. Tobias hit the first Hork-Bajir at about fifty miles an hour. He swooped away, leaving the alien clutching at the slimy mess where his eyes used to be.

That was all Cassie needed. She broke away and ran back down the pier.

I finally got there and went after the remaining Hork-Bajir-Controller.

<Morph!> I yelled to Cassie. <Morph and head back for the stairs!>

She looked at the other humans and Hork-Bajir behind her in the line. "Run! All of you, run!"

They did. Cassie plowed into the panicky crowd. Moments later a black-maned head appeared above the shoulders of the crowd. Cassie had become a horse and was racing for the stairs.

I started after her, racing back around the pool toward Marco, Rachel, Tom, and the crowd of hosts they'd freed from the cages.

The Controllers were starting to get organized. A group of Taxxons were slithering out to stop Cassie and me. Both the Hork-Bajir and the Taxxons were carrying weapons now.

<Up and over!> I said to Cassie as we neared the line of Taxxons.

<Up and over!> she yelled back.

I leaped. Cassie jumped. Side by side, we sailed over the startled Taxxons. They fired their handheld Dracon beams, but too late. The beams sizzled the air behind us and we blew past.

I could see Rachel's towering gray bulk just ahead. The stairs were near. I saw Marco with Tom.

We were going to make it!

And then *he* stepped out daintily from a group of Hork-Bajir.

He seemed almost harmless in his Andalite body. A gentle half deer, half human—looking creature with bluish fur and an extra set of eyes on comical stalks.

Visser Three didn't look all that scary. Not compared to the Hork-Bajir, the Taxxons, or even our own Earth-animals.

But Visser Three had an Andalite body. He had an Andalite's power to morph. And he had been all over the universe acquiring the genetic patterns of monsters like nothing ever seen on Earth.

A Taxxon slithered up beside Visser Three and spoke. It was a weird, half-whistling sound. *"Ssssweer trrreeesswew eeeesstrew."*

Visser Three said nothing. He just looked at me with the horizontal slits that were his eyes.

<This Taxxon fool says you are wild animals,> Visser Three said. <He wants to know if he and his brothers can eat you.> He laughed silently. <But I know you are not animals. I know who and what you are. So. Not all of you Andalites died when I burned your ship.>

It took me a couple of seconds to realize what he meant. Then it hit me. Of course! He thought we were Andalites. He'd guessed that we were morphs, not real animals. And he knew that the Andalites were the only species with morphing technology.

<I compliment you on getting this far. But it will accomplish nothing. Because now, my brave Andalite warriors, it is time. Time to die.>

He began to morph.

<I acquired this body on the fourth moon of the second planet of a dying star. Like it?>

I realized I'd been wrong to be hopeful.

We were not going to make it.

CHAPTER 26

From Visser Three's Andalite body, the creature grew. Tall as a tree, towering over even Rachel. Eight massive legs. Eight long, spindly arms, each ending in a three-fingered claw. And from the place where the top set of arms grew came the heads.

Heads. Plural. Eight of them. This creature had a thing for the number eight.

Even the Hork-Bajir-Controllers backed away. Even they didn't want to be near Visser Three when he morphed this way.

But the Taxxons edged in closer, crowding around

their leader like a pack of hungry dogs looking for table scraps.

I was frozen in terror. Stunned. Even the tiger that was a part of me was confused and worried.

I had started to think that with our morphed bodies we could take on anything. But we couldn't take on this monster. Not and survive.

<Run!> I yelled to the others. <Up the stairs!>

Cassie nudged two of the humans from the cages and tossed back her head. They figured out what she wanted and climbed on her back. Then she galloped toward the stairs.

<Yes, run,> Visser Three crowed. <It makes a more challenging target.>

Then, Visser Three struck.

From one of the heads a round, spinning ball of flame erupted. A ball of flame that flew like a missile.

It skimmed through the air and splatted against the back of one of the women riding Cassie.

"Ahhhh!" She fell off, screaming and rolling around to put out the flames. Cassie kept going with only one rider. She reached the base of the stairs.

<Target practice!> Visser Three laughed. He fired fireball after fireball, one head after another.

One singed my shoulder and flew past. One hit Rachel in the ear and made her scream in my head and trumpet in terror.

The air was full of fire.

<We have to get out of here!> Marco yelled.

<Yes, run! Run for the stairs!> I repeated. <Rachel! Get moving! Clear a path!>

A big swarm of us was heading for the stairs, but the Taxxons had closed in around us. Anyone that got away from Visser Three was swarmed over by the Taxxons.

I saw Tom out of the corner of my eye. He was swinging his fists at a pair of Taxxons that were circling around him. Tom couldn't hurt them, but he was trying just the same.

Rachel ran over and plowed into one of them, crushing him beneath her tree-trunk legs. Marco threw his arms around the second Taxxon and twisted till it split open, spilling its putrid guts all over the floor.

Rachel had hit the bottom few stairs and stopped. Elephant bodies are great for some things. But they are useless for climbing stairs.

<Morph back!> I told Rachel.

She began to shrink almost immediately, but there wasn't time to wait until the morphing was complete. Rachel started up the stairs as a shifting mass of gray and pink, part human, part elephant, staggering on weird, half-finished legs and dragging a shriveled trunk that made her pretty face into something awful to see.

We ran. But it was impossible.

By the time we had climbed a few dozen stairs, there were only a few free humans and two free Hork-Bajir with us. The rest had all been recaptured or burned.

A fireball exploded at my feet and I snarled. But still we retreated.

We were a hundred feet up the stairs when the last two freed Hork-Bajir were brought down by the Visser's fireballs. They fell in flames.

The Visser was climbing the stairs now, all alone. He was so big he barely fit on the stairs. I knew when we reached the point where the walls closed in around the stairs that we would be safe from Visser Three. Glancing up, I saw that Cassie was almost to safety above us, with one human rider.

The rest of us, along with Tom and a pitiful handful of freed humans, were bunched together.

Visser Three began pelting the staircase ahead of us with fire. We were trapped. Fire ahead. Visser Three himself behind.

"No," I heard a familiar voice say. "No, you filthy creep. You aren't going to win this time."

It was Tom.

All alone, he charged at Visser Three, armed with nothing but his fists.

One of the Visser's arms came down and swung at him.

<Tom!> I cried. My tiger body roared with all its might. But the sound was lost in the noise of crying humans and whistling Taxxons.

I saw Tom stagger from the Visser's blow.

I saw him fall from the edge of the stairs.

I went a little crazy.

I was on the Visser before I knew what was happening. On him, digging my claws into his flesh. I twisted up and behind one of his eight heads.

The tiger in me knew what to do. I sank my teeth into his neck and clamped my powerful jaws and held on.

Another head turned back and aimed a fireball at me. I dodged the first fireball. The second burned my flank. I jumped clear.

The Visser roared in pain. I roared in hatred.

And we ran, ran, ran up those stairs with a hundred nightmares on our heels.

CHAPTER 27

We ran. Exhausted and burned and terrified, we ran.

Visser Three had made one mistake. He was too large in his morph to follow us much farther up the stairs.

I heard Visser Three yell something as we finally got away. He said, <I'll kill you all, Andalites. Run away, it doesn't matter! I'll kill you all!>.

Actually, I think it did matter. We hadn't exactly destroyed Visser Three, but we had come out of it alive, we Animorphs.

The final count was exactly one human freed—the

woman who rode Cassie's back up out of that hellish pit.

And Cassie had gotten away clean. It had been the suspicious Controller policeman who had grabbed her. He was the only Controller to know her name, where she lived, and that she had been spying on The Sharing.

Cassie said we didn't have to worry about him anymore. She didn't want to talk about what had happened to him.

As for Tom . . . My brother.

Tom was not freed.

I was lying in my bed, shaking and shivering and crying from the aftereffects of terror, when I heard him come home later that night.

He never knew that I was the tiger. He never knew how close I had come to freeing him. He was a Controller again. The Yeerk was in his head once more.

Cassie and Marco and Rachel and I had all made it up those stairs. We had emerged into the hallway of a school that would never seem the same to us again.

And Tobias? He survived, too.

It was almost morning when I was awakened from dead sleep by feathery beating on my window.

I opened it and Tobias flew in.

"You made it," I said. "Oh, man, you had me scared. I figured you were still trapped down there. I mean, I thought you could probably find somewhere to hide in that cavern, but I knew you'd been morphed for a long time. I was worried you wouldn't be able to morph back without getting caught. It's good to see you."

<Good to see you, too, Jake,> he said. <How are the others?>

"Alive," I said. "Alive. I guess that's all that counts."

<Yes. That is all that matters.>

"Come on, Tobias," I said. "Morph back. You can stay here. I'll even let you have the bed. I could sleep on nails, I'm so tired."

He didn't say anything. And I guess in my heart I'd known it all along. I just didn't want to admit it.

"Come on, Tobias," I said again. "Morph back."

<Jake . . .>

"Just come on, back to human now, dude. No more flying tonight."

<I hid in the cavern for a while,> he said. <They didn't see me. But I had to stay out of sight till I could get out. Jake . . . it took too long. Too long. More than two hours.>

I just stared at him. At his laser-focus eyes, at his

wicked beak and sharp talons. And at his wings. At the broad, powerful wings that let him fly.

<I guess this is me from now on,> Tobias said.

I knew there were tears falling down my cheeks, but I didn't care anymore.

<It's okay, Jake. Like you said, we're alive.>

I went to the window and looked up at the stars. Somewhere up there, around one of those cold, twinkling stars, was the Andalite home world. Somewhere up there was . . . hope.

<They'll come,> Tobias said. <The Andalites will come. And until then . . .>

I nodded and wiped away my tears. "Yeah," I said. "Until then, we fight."

<LEARN THE TRUTH.>
Don't miss

ANIMORPHS™ #02

THE
VISITOR

Part of me just wanted to run. Even a hologram of Visser Three makes your skin crawl. But now that he had figured out it wasn't real, the cat part of me was just bored.

I realized why I could hear Visser Three—the hologram projector must not be able to transmit thought-speech. It translated it into regular speech.

"Is there progress on locating the Andalite bandits?"

"No, Visser. Nothing yet."

I knew who he meant by "Andalite bandits." That was us, the Animorphs.

"I want them found. I want them found NOW!"

Chapman jumped back in surprise at the Visser's command. I could smell fear on him.

In a calmer tone, Visser Three continued. "This

cannot go on, Iniss Two-Two-Six, it cannot go on. The Council of Thirteen will hear of it. They will wonder why I reported to them that all Andalite ships near this planet had been destroyed and all the Andalites killed. They will be suspicious. They will be angry. And when the Council of Thirteen is angry with me, I am angry with you."

Chapman was literally quivering. I smelled human sweat. And I smelled something else. Something not totally human. It was very faint . . . was that the Yeerk itself I was smelling? Was I smelling the Yeerk slug in Chapman's head?

It seemed impossible. But there was some strange smell. Something . . . something . . . I concentrated all my cat mind on analyzing the smell.

"What is *that*?"

Chapman swiveled in his chair.

I looked up and froze. Chapman was staring right at me. And worse, much worse, Visser Three's stalk eyes were focused on me, too.

"It's called a cat," Chapman said nervously. "An Earth species used as a pet. The humans keep them close and find comfort in them."

"Why is it in here?"

"It belongs to the girl. My . . . the host's daughter."

"I see," Visser Three said. "Well, kill it. Kill it immediately."

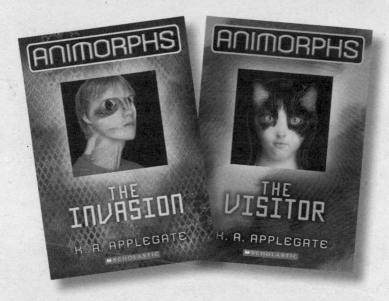

ANIMORPHS™

SAVING THE WORLD WILL CHANGE YOU.

The invasion begins in this action-packed series! Keep reading to discover the fate of the Animorphs.

■SCHOLASTIC

Create your own morph at
www.scholastic.com/morph

SCHOLASTIC and associated logos
are trademarks and/or registered
trademarks of Scholastic Inc.

AMORPH1